Viviane Mo   A
photographer at 19, she later became a freelance
writer, and has contributed to various European
magazines. Her great knowledge of France in the
Middle Ages has led her to write quite a number of
detective novels, all set in the twelfth century.

By Viviane Moore

Blue Blood
A Black Romance
The Darkest Red

A BLACK ROMANCE

Viviane Moore

Translated by
Rory Mulholland

ORION

An Orion paperback

First published in Great Britain in 2000
by Victor Gollancz
This paperback edition published in 2001
by Orion Books Ltd,
Orion House, 5 Upper St Martin's Lane,
London WC2H 9EA

A CIP catalogue record for this book
is available from the British Library.

ISBN 0 75284 417 2

Printed and bound in Great Britain by
Clays Ltd, St Ives plc

For Suzanne, this voyage to the twelfth century that together we dreamed of.

to Landivisiau

Roman road

to Carhaix

N

Broerac's camp

Wild boars' pool

Chaos

Génovéfa's farm

Cave

Arched Rock

Abyss

Huelgoat

Ninian's lake

The mine

The Hills of Arez in the Twelfth Century

Peter McClure 2000

Prologue

A ghostly sun pierced the fog that hung over the hills of Arez. Purple heather stained the rocky crests, while the clusters of tall trees and the marsh of Yeûn remained in shadow. A black sludge oozed from the eviscerated peat bog, and unwholesome vapours floated through the gorse, above the stagnant waters.

On this September morning in the year 1144, Renoulf and his son Maloù had left home at dawn in the hope of poaching game to enrich the pot. The two men moved slowly, paying no heed to the swarms of mosquitos that assailed them. They waded through knee-deep water, probing the thick mud in the potholes. From time to time they disturbed a coot, and its cry rattled out from among the reeds.

Small and thickset, Renoulf wore over his tunic a dogskin cape tied roughly with a piece of rope. His grey eyes were two spatters of mist below his low forehead, and his face was lined with wrinkles. He was a man who said little. When he did speak, it was always with downcast eyes, as though the bog that surrounded him had imprisoned his spirit.

Maloù was squat and robust like his father. He was sixteen years old, yet words and wit were still strangers to him, and he liked nothing better than to spend entire days tracking the beasts of Yeûn.

He knew the dangers of the vast swamp so well that the rector of Lannédern often sought him out to guide him to Youdik, a great pool of murky green water that bubbled and seethed and let off foul odours. Wise old folk said that Youdik was the gate of darkness, the gaping mouth that led to Hell. Only a man of God could safely take the souls of the damned to that place, sewn up in the skin of a black dog or of a wolf.

The sun had just passed Menez Mikêl and the men had only three more snares to check, one of them on the bank of the river Elez.

'You go to the Elez, Maloù, and I will go to Yeûn. We will meet back at the house,' the father's muffled voice growled.

The son nodded, turned on his heels and, with a determined air, took a grassy path which he knew led to the river. As he drew closer to his destination, the fog grew ever thicker, hovering in dense bands a few inches above the ground.

All was silent now. Neither the birds nor the wind could be heard, and the sound of the young man's footsteps was smothered by the enveloping fog. Every rock, every tree trunk twisted and writhed in front of him. Disorientated, Maloù stopped and raised his nose like a dog sniffing out a trail. His nostrils flared as he turned his head from left to right, seeking out the sour smell of the Elez amid the stench of decomposition that emanated from the marsh.

He could not find it. He knelt down, put his ear to the sodden earth and listened, motionless, alert to subterranean sounds. Then he stood up, reached for his staff and moved off to the right, silently parting the long grass.

The mist had become so thick that Maloù could no longer make out his own feet, but on hearing the faint murmur of water flowing over rocks he knew he must be close by.

The gaunt silhouette of a dead tree rose up suddenly before him. Maloù recognised the tortured trunk as one of the markers he used to help him find his traps. His snare, hidden in the rushes along the bank, could not be far away.

He turned again to the right, towards the sound of the fast-flowing water, and then stumbled as his staff struck something that looked like the remains of an animal. He could barely see it through the fog, so he turned it carefully with his foot. As he did so, the thing was seized by a fierce spasm that flung it through the tall grass onto the muddy bank.

Maloù jumped back. But the creature, half submerged in the water, had stopped moving. He waited a while, but nothing happened. He moved closer, his staff held high in readiness, to see what animal confronted him.

He gasped, for what he had taken for a dead beast was the muddy body of a child.

Maloù bent down, took hold of the corpse under the armpits and pulled it out of the water and across to the foot of the old tree. He carefully wiped the child's face, brushing aside the dirty hair and scratching off the mud and grass with his nails to see if he recognised it. The child was no more than eight or nine years old. The blank eyes stared at Maloù, the mouth gaping open with teeth bared.

Maloù stood up abruptly, and marched off through the gorse bushes to look for his snare. He and his father were to deliver some peat that day, and he knew that Renoulf did not like to be kept waiting. He returned a few minutes later with a coot hanging from his gamebag, picked up the child's body, threw it over his shoulder and trudged off along the path to Yeûn.

The house where Maloù and his parents lived was on one of the muddy paths that led to the marsh of Yeûn. The marsh was rich in fish and waterfowl, and from June to September supplied the nearby villages with all the peat they required. Maloù's family was one of four that eked out their living from the Yeûn. Each worked their own peat bog, and mostly kept themselves to themselves.

A bramble hedge circled the hovel, which appeared to remain standing by miracle alone, its cob walls threatening to collapse at any moment. Thick curls of smoke billowed out through a hole in the rush roof. It was here that Maloù was born, and here that he and his family still lived, clinging to the edge of the marsh that fed them.

There were five of them in the miserable shack: Turold Ar Moigne, the grandfather, Renoulf and Gaïdik, the parents, and Maloù and his little sister Katik.

Renoulf, like his father before him, worked the peat bogs of the Yeûn. From early summer till autumn the family set out daily for the bogs at dawn. Renoulf and Maloù made long gashes in the turf with their blades and from these cut sods the size of bricks. Gaïdik and Katik then, with much difficulty, carried the damp slabs to their cart, which they hauled to a spot near their house, and there it was little Katik's task to stack the sods in a pile to dry.

Old Turold usually stayed at home now, ever since a hound belonging to the Lord of Huelgoat had bitten off his right arm. Sometimes he would help the two women, but his favourite activity was fishing for trout along the banks of the Elez or stretching out on the grass and snoozing beside his fishing rod.

If it was a good summer the turf would dry quickly and could be loaded up and brought to Huelgoat, to Saint-Herbot or to Lannédern. But if the summer was a wet one, the dark months of winter would often arrive before the sods had dried.

These few trips in the overflowing cart were the only contact the two men had with people from outside the marsh. As for the women, they remained captives of the immense sadness of the Yeûn. Their only link to the outside world was when, once or twice a year, Père Gwen came from the church at Lannédern to remind them how to pray.

Renoulf, who had just taken off his outer leggings, gave a start when Maloù kicked open the door. It was dark in the hovel, but light enough to show that what his son carried on his shoulder was a human form.

'What have you got there, you wretch?'

With the back of his hand Maloù moved aside two bowls and gently placed the body on the slab of stone upon which the family took their meals. Renoulf leaned over to take a look.

'Another one. Where did you find it? Huh, Maloù? And why did you bring him here? The lad's well gone, you should have buried him.'

Maloù whimpered sheepishly.

'All right, all right,' said his father. 'Go and get the mule, I'll tell Gaïdik. We'll take him to Père Gwen along with the peat.'

PART ONE

Death, and Judgement, and cold Hell; remem-
    bering there, then man must fear.
Foolish is the man of unreflective spirit.
For he must die.

Inscription on the Breton ossuary of La Martyre

1

It was now three months since Galeran de Lesneven had left Saint-Denis. He departed on the twelfth day of June, the day after Abbé Suger inaugurated the great cathedral in the presence of Queen Aliénor of Aquitaine, King Louis VII and all the kingdom's nobility.

Suger had become a close friend, but the knight was weary of the court and its intrigues and wanted to return to his home, as he put it, at 'the far end of the world'. But he promised the Abbot he would return to Saint-Denis the following spring.

Galeran was from Léon in Brittany. He had not been home in almost five years, and now longed to see the manor where he had spent his childhood. His mother welcomed him with the familiar smile he so loved. She had changed little in all the time he had been away, and looked much younger than most Breton women of her years, as though her Gascon roots protected her from ageing. Even the harshness and the cold of Léon's rude climate had failed to grey her thick brown hair or to add any wrinkles to her happy face except those she'd gained through laughter. She had lost several children when they were still no more than infants, but she thanked God for the three that had grown up healthy and strong, and for a good and loyal husband.

Arzhel, her youngest, was now sixteen years old. She had left home a year ago to become a companion to Duchess Ermengarde, the mother of Conan III, Duke of Cornwall. Her eldest son Ronan was in the south, somewhere between Aquitaine and Castille, and she had no news of him. Swarthy and capricious, he felt more at home near the Mediterranean than on the edge of the cold northern ocean.

But now Galeran was home again, and Dame Mathilde was happy to see the son who, although she would not admit it even to herself, was her favourite.

Calm and composed as always, Gilduin de Lesneven embraced his son. Gilduin was now more used to supervising work in the fields or watching over livestock than waging war. Hard-working and respected by all, he was also a wise man, to whom noble and peasant alike would come for counsel.

Gilduin had had his manor rebuilt with granite slabs after a fire burned down the stables and took the lives of two of his workers. It was a costly business, but the Vicomte de Léon, Guiomarch III, to whom he had rendered many services, had helped him out by supplying him with skilled masons and several cartloads of cut stone. This generosity Gilduin owed to an important agreement he had brokered between the Duke of Cornwall, Conan III, and the viscounty of Léon, which had facilitated the transport of salt from the marsh of Guérande. The precious crystals were now carted to Quimper under the protection of Conan III and then on to Léon by the men of Guiomarch. This was one example among many of Gilduin's negotiation skills.

The old wooden keep had thus been dismantled, and a stone tower now rose up in its place. Only the outer stone walls had yet to be completed. The farmyard had been enlarged, and the moat filled in to allow for bigger outbuildings. Now there was a forge, an oven for baking bread, a byre, and three wooden houses where the men-at-arms and the farmhands lived. The new stables could accommodate thirty horses.

It was not without pride that Gilduin took his son on a tour of the new tower. In thirty years he had rebuilt this château, which had fallen into disrepair after his father, Florent de Lesneven, had practically ruined the family by participating in the first Crusade.

Galeran, for his part, was simply glad to be among his own again, and to have about him some childhood friends, many of whom now had children of their own. He spent his time hunting and fishing, and in the evenings would relax by the hearth with his parents. He relished these moments of intimacy when they sat plunged deep in thought or launched into some tale of heroic deeds. Dame Mathilde, who had heard the stories a hundred times before, would hum to herself as she wound wool around her osier distaff.

But happy as he was here, after a few weeks Galeran began to hanker after the solitude of the shores where he had wandered as a child.

The weather was fine. September was almost at an end, but the warmth of the summer looked as if it would last until well into October. Galeran left home at dawn, and after two hours' riding across the moor reached a long white beach.

Quolibet, his six-year-old gelding, more used to riding into combat than to pleasure trips, balked a little at the loose, damp soil of the shoreline. Galeran dismounted and led him by the bridle towards the ruins of an old chapel perched on top of a dune. He stood there, his back to the wind, and surveyed the ocean that rose and fell before him. A school of whales frolicked near the water's edge.

The knight tied his horse to a tree stump. Then he stood and stretched, filling his lungs with the sharp air that bore the acrid perfume he loved. He had always felt at home here, on these dunes where priests once tended bonfires that after many years had to be extinguished because of ever more frequent and ferocious Viking raids. The coast, which long before had been illuminated by Roman beacons, once again returned to darkness.

A little stone fort had housed lookouts who would scan the horizon and raise the alarm if an attack was imminent. The building was later transformed into a chapel. This had twice burned down and been rebuilt, but now lay abandoned, sinking slowly into the dunes among the thistles and the long grass.

Galeran stepped over the charred planks that were all that remained of the door that led into the empty building. Black marks left by the fire disfigured the walls, and at the back stood a broken altar. On the ground in front of him was a long rectangular flagstone. He knelt down beside it and with an impatient hand brushed aside the sand that covered an escutcheon, the shield of the Lesnevens, that had been engraved on the stone.

Here lay the first in the line of descent, an ancestor who had met his death fighting off a Viking attack. But family legend had it that the vault was empty, for only those Lesnevens who died in peace could rest in peace.

Galeran, who believed wholeheartedly in God's infinite indulgence, invoked Saint Michel, that warrior archangel whose job it is to judge souls. After all, these were violent times, and one could no longer easily distinguish the wheat from the chaff. The knight's ancestor was somewhere between the two, and given the obstinacy of his race might well have been able to slip in through the gates of Heaven.

Galeran got to his feet again, his soul appeased. He stopped at the doorstep of the chapel and looked out again at the ocean. The whales had disappeared and the tide was going out, leaving behind it long lines of brown seaweed.

It was here one stormy summer night that Galeran had watched the beautiful Auan emerge naked from the waves. It was here he had taken her in his arms, covering her pearly skin with a thousand kisses. In the warm dunes the expert Auan showed him how to make love, and together they watched the morning star rise up in the sky. Galeran was fifteen years old, Auan twenty and a widow. He never saw her again, and had never forgotten her. He later learned that she had offered herself to all who came her way before eventually shutting herself away in a convent, where her piety came to be greatly admired.

Galeran smiled at the memory of Auan rolling in the dunes, laughingly leaving the ephemeral imprint of her splendid body in the sand.

'Perhaps that is eternity,' he thought as he got back into the saddle. 'I would like to die here on his magical beach where the dead and the living mingle so freely.'

He turned and decided to gallop as far as Aber Wrac'h. There he loosened his grip on the reins and let his steed follow the paths that led over the short grass of the moor. Seagulls followed him overhead, piercing the air with their shrill cries.

Galeran had barely passed over the drawbridge of the manor when the tall figure of Gilduin rushed out to meet him, accompanied by a man he did not recognise.

'My son, this fellow tells me he has a message for you from his master. He has orders to speak only with you.'

'Very well, Father.'

The stranger watched them silently. He was small and thickset, with crooked legs, and over his chain mail wore a studded belt from which hung a battleaxe. His eyes, small and deep set like those of a monkey, were barely visible between his dense eyebrows and the thick beard that covered his cheeks.

'I am Galeran de Lesneven,' said the knight. 'Who has sent you and what do you want?'

The man bowed, almost reluctantly, and spoke in a husky voice.

'My name is Thustan, sir, and I come from the hills of Arez.'

Apparently not a man much used to speaking, he drew his breath before continuing.

'My master, Broérec de Huelgoat, sends me to fetch you to his manor. Here is his message.'

He took out from under his tunic a parchment which he handed to Galeran, then went to sit cross-legged on the ground next to his horse. He removed the axe from his belt, placing it in front of him. Gilduin frowned as he watched him, then turned to his son. Galeran, who had now read the parchment, looked up at him.

'What does this Broérec want with you, my son? Weren't you at his side during that strange war between Conan III and Robert de Vitré?'

Galeran was pensive, his thoughts on the last time, some ten years before, that he had seen Broérec de Huelgoat.

'A strange war indeed! It was in 1134, I had just turned seventeen, and I had offered my services to the Duke of Cornwall. After ten long years of fighting he had just taken the fortress of Vitré, and his goal now was to hang on to it. But Robert de Vitré had other plans.'

'He got what he wanted in the end,' said Gilduin.

'What do you mean, Father?'

'You know that Victome Guiomarch honours me by seeking my advice, and that I regularly meet with him at his château.'

'Yes, Father. But what did he say to you?'

'He told me of this affair. It appears that Conan simply wearied of the interminable battle. For ten years Vitré, his former comrade-in-arms, had been fighting him. But after Conan finally took the town, Robert won it back again in just a few weeks. No one knows how he managed it, but undoubtedly there was treachery involved. And the Duke did not raise a finger to take it back!'

'What about his knights?'

'He abandoned them. Although he did, on the advice of his mother, Ermengarde, propose to buy a few of them back.'

'Ten years of war for that! I am not surprised his supporters lost faith in him. Did the Vicomte speak to you of Broérec?'

'He did not. But what does Broérec say in his message?'

'He writes of a great danger facing him and his family, and in the name of loyalty asks for my help.'

'And what does he mean by that?'

'He is reminding me that I am beholden to him. Broérec

14

once saved my life when I was ambushed, and now he wants me to pay my debt.'

The scar that ran across Galeran's forehead seemed to deepen as though under the strain of some intense effort.

'I shall have to leave you, Father,' he said.

'I understand, but I see you are not happy about this.'

'Father, it is my duty. He is a brother-in-arms. We are linked by blood, even if we do not see eye to eye. In Broérec, as in all of us, there is both good and bad.'

'I fear badness has the upper hand with him,' Gilduin said sombrely. 'His conduct is not that of a Christian knight. I have heard he leads a wicked life, and I can well believe it looking at that beanpole he sent here!'

Gilduin looked with some pride at his son. The knight was tall, his hair so short it was hard to make out that it was black, and his open face changed expression as quickly as the Breton sea.

'What did you yourself make of Broérec?' Gilduin asked.

'He was a strange companion. He was eight years my elder, and a man of letters who did not lack spirit. But he conducted his war more like a peasant than a knight. In fact, he liked the war for the very fact that it was a peasant war. Ambushes, traps, attacks at night . . . Broérec knew the lie of the land better than any of Vitré's men. Yes, in truth, he made a very odd companion.'

2

At dawn the knight rose and put on his long purple tunic and his coat of chain mail. He fixed the heavy shoulder-strap that bore his sword and tied his shield over his back. A farmhand brought him a caparisoned Quolibet and the knight hung his gamebag, his goatskin and his dagger on the pommel.

Dame Mathilde, who could not hold back her tears, appeared with her husband to bid their son farewell. Galeran embraced his parents, then mounted his steed and rode off alongside Thustan without turning to look back.

Thustan had not said a word since the previous day, and Galeran, watching him from the corner of his eye, had no doubt the man would make a poor travelling companion.

He had consulted his father's geographical tables, a long roll made up of twelve parchments copied from a Roman map, and decided to take one of the Roman roads that led to Carhaix before turning off towards Huelgoat. Once they had left the ancient highway he would have to trust Thustan to guide him through the marshes and vast forests that surrounded the hills of Arez. The region they were about to enter was one of the wildest in Brittany. There were few towns, and fewer roads. The hills of Arez and Ar Menez Reûn Dû were notorious for the roughness of their inhabitants. The forests were deep and the legends legion.

Determined to arrive before nightfall, Galeran made a sign to the man at his side and spurred on his horse.

The sun was already high in the sky when the knight ordered Thustan to stop to let the horses drink some water, and so that they themselves could eat. It looked like a good place to make a halt, with a stream running nearby and a copse to

16

provide shade. Thustan tied his horse to a tree and went to urinate on the Roman road. Galeran smiled as he watched him. Like many of his compatriots, the man liked to show his contempt for the former occupiers of Armorica.

After a quick look around, the knight dismounted and placed his shield at the foot of a tree. When he turned around Thustan had vanished, and only his horse was to be seen, calmly eating whatever grass it could reach from its tether.

Galeran frowned. He could hear the murmur of water under the moss. He looked along the road, marked here and there with a twisted tree, but there was not a soul to be seen. A crafty fellow indeed, he thought to himself.

Taking his horse by the bridle, he went and filled his goatskin in the brook. Thustan was there when he returned, lighting a fire, and with a bundle of bloody fur at his feet. He had cut the rabbit's head off with his axe.

'Good job,' said Galeran, taking out his knife. 'See to the horses. I'll prepare the rabbit.'

Thustan did not reply. He blew one last time on the twigs and placed a piece of bark over them which immediately caught fire. Then he stood up and began rubbing down the horses with tufts of grass. When he had finished he led them to the stream, where he left them to wander freely and drink their fill. Galeran sat on a stone and watched him. Thustan held his blue eyes for a moment, then looked away towards a rocky point on the horizon.

'The Roc'h Trevezel, the Yeûn . . .'

'The March of Yeûn? The marsh of hell?'

Thustan nodded, and came and sat near Galeran. The knight opened his gamebag and handed him a chunk of bread and a large onion.

'Eat this,' he said. 'Tell me a little about yourself. Were you at Vitré with your master?'

Thustan's face hardened, and not another word came from his lips. He sat chewing his meat and staring at the axe he had placed on the ground before him. Galeran knew he would get no more from him, and he too silently resumed his meal.

He reread Broérec's enigmatic message and wondered what could constitute danger for a man of his ilk. He considered the matter as he sat back against a tree, sharpening his knife and watching his companion gnaw at the bones of the rabbit.

When he had gleaned the last pieces of meat from the carcass, Thustan took some grass and wiped the blood from his knife. He hummed an old war song whose melody the knight recognised. He was undoubtedly a warrior, a man who delighted only in seeing the red life force gush from the open arteries of his enemies.

Galeran sheathed his dagger and called to him.

'Let us go, Thustan. You will soon be home. Fetch the horses.'

Thustan jumped to his feet, slid his axe into his belt and went to find the horses, who had wandered off along the brook. While he did so, Galeran put out the fire and covered the ashes and the remains of the rabbit with earth and leaves. He calculated that the château was no more than five or six leagues away.

He patted Quolibet's neck, climbed up onto the saddle and rode off with Thustan at his side towards the Roc'h Trevezel and Huelgoat.

3

The two men had put a league between them and the Roman road that led to Carhaix. Thustan said it was time to head into the forest. He manoeuvred his robust little horse ahead of Quolibet and took the lead without hesitation. He was on home ground. They took a narrow path that cut through tall ferns.

The forest of hundred-year-old oaks, pine and ash trees had kept its primeval darkness. The tree trunks intertwined like the columns of a cathedral, and daylight barely pierced the canopy. The paths were blocked here and there with large rocks.

Galeran found this place, which the hand of man had not yet domesticated, very gloomy after the open skies of the moor.

Thustan slowed his pace. The path was becoming narrower and narrower, and brambles tore at the men's breeches and the horses' legs. Night was approaching.

A distant screech made the horses whinny. A guttural cry, from much closer, came in response. Thustan muttered and spurred on his mount. Galeran put his hand on his sword. The horses were nervous, their ears pricked up.

Suddenly there came a crashing sound from the undergrowth and a giant of a man, a sheepskin thrown over his broad shoulders, stood before them, blocking their path. Galeran saw movement in the bushes on either side of the track and knew the fellow was not alone.

'Where are you off to, then, Thustan?' asked the giant, ignoring Galeran. 'Back to your devil of a master, like a scurvy dog?'

His voice was hoarse, and the look on his face did not bode well.

Thustan gave a savage yell, reached for his axe, and was about to leap at the man when Galeran grabbed him by the shoulder to restrain him.

'Stay where you are, Thustan!'

His tone brooked no reply, and Thustan stopped with a grumble. Galeran turned to the giant.

'Who are you and what do you want of us?' he asked calmly.

'And you, sir, what are you doing on my land?' came the insolent response.

'On your land?'

'Yes, my land. This forest and all that surrounds it is my domain. And let anyone who dares gainsay me.'

'Well then, since I am dealing with a lord, allow me to introduce myself. I am Galeran de Lesneven. And what is your name?'

The man's face tensed.

'Hoël de Huelgoat, at your service, sir,' he said arrogantly, drawing himself up to his full height.

Thustan clenched his fists, but did not move.

Galeran looked at the giant's face, and saw that it was both refined and youthful. Despite his great build, the knight reckoned he could not be more than eighteen years old.

'I know of only one Lord of Huelgoat,' he said firmly.

The man's face turned a deep red.

'That one's neither man nor lord, but a demon! I would turn back now if that's where you're headed.'

Thustan growled like an animal on a chain.

'Do not move, do you hear me?' the knight snapped at him.

Then he turned again to the giant.

'I couldn't even if I wanted to. I have a debt to pay, and if you are the man I think you are, then you will understand.'

The giant hesitated, peering at the knight's face through the gloom.

'I shall let you pass on two conditions.'

'And what are they?'

'That you do not forget me when you have reached Broérec's château, and that you will meet again with me if I request it.'

The knight nodded his agreement.

'Very well, Hoël de Huelgoat. Now, let us pass.'

But the man had already disappeared into the undergrowth.

'I'll kill the dog!' cried Thustan.

'Ah, found your tongue again? So you know the chap?'

But Thustan had already retreated into his usual silence.

'Well, he clearly knows you, and he knows your master! All this is starting to get my blood up. Now get moving and take me to Broérec before I lose my temper.'

Thustan whipped his horse and rode off, followed closely by the knight. The path soon grew wider and the two men were able to ride side by side. They left the forest and arrived at the foot of a hill covered in grey rocks and brambles. Thustan pointed at a high stone wall ringed by a moat.

'That is where Sir Broérec lives.'

A large oak drawbridge, its beams cased in iron, blocked access to the château. Broérec had built his castle on the site of an old Roman camp – Galeran recognised the work of the Romans in the placing and pointing of the stones. The site was ideal for a stronghold. The slopes leading up to it were abrupt, the area around was clear of trees, and from the top of the tower it was possible to see for some twenty leagues in all directions.

4

The two men rode slowly towards the château and stopped some twenty yards before the entrance. Thustan took the horn that hung from his saddle and gave three long blasts, in response to which came three short notes from within the walls.

They had been seen while still a long way off, and already there were shouts inside the château and the sound of many feet running to and fro.

Galeran looked around him as he waited for the drawbridge to be lowered. Not far from him was a gallows from which swung the corpse of an emaciated old man.

'Just like Broérec to leave this sort of warning,' he mused.

He guided his horse towards the gallows for a closer look. The execution appeared to have been fairly recent, for the crows had not yet picked off all the flesh, and the wretch's face was still intact. His tattered tunic and worn breeches suggested his existence had been a miserable one.

'Show yourselves,' shouted a guard from the battlements.

'It's me, Thustan. What are you playing at, you filthy good-for-nothing. Go and get Sir Broérec and open up for us, and quick, you scoundrel!'

The man did not reply to Thustan's insults, but soon chains began to creak as the drawbridge was slowly lowered.

As Galeran and Thustan rode onto the bridge the knight heard a whistling sound he had heard too many times before, and instinctively pressed his body down against his horse's neck. But the message was evidently addressed to Thustan, for a long arrow fledged in white struck a post next to his head.

'Quickly!' cried Thustan. 'Pull it up, you dogs!'

'A warm welcome indeed,' said Galeran when they had

reached the courtyard and the drawbridge protected them from the outside world. 'That must have been a little sign from the friendly chap we met in the forest. Just who are you at war with, Thustan?'

'With the peasants, my friend. With "my" peasants,' replied a voice that Galeran recognised immediately.

Broérec, the Lord of Huelgoat, stood before him, his long blond hair blowing about his shoulders. He wore a black tunic and a coat of chain mail, and carried at his side his favourite weapon, a Saracen scimitar with its deadly curved blade. Many years of war had not changed this giant of a man. But he now bore on his left cheek a long scar that Galeran had not seen before. He was thirty-five years of age, as blond as a Dane, and easily as tall as the pretender the knight had encountered in the forest. Only his dark eyes and severe air showed his Armorican roots. There was a strange charm about him which his looks alone could not account for.

'*Homme fatal, homme de guerre,*' thought Galeran as he considered him.

'I knew you would come, Galeran. As soon as I heard you were at your father's château . . .'

'How did you know?'

'That does not matter,' he replied haughtily.

'What does matter is that you explain to me what is going on here,' retorted Galeran.

'I see you are still a tetchy devil.'

Galeran gave Broérec a severe look.

'Very well,' said Broérec, his tone more abrupt now. 'If that is how we are to play, then so be it. Follow me.'

A score of men-at-arms went about their business in the large courtyard, which sheltered several wooden huts and a stable. Galeran reluctantly entrusted Quolibet to a ragged boy, who led him off towards the drinking troughs. A covered cistern occupied the centre of the parade ground. A high palisade and a second moat protected the fortified tower where Broérec lived, which could be reached via a wooden footbridge and another drawbridge. The Lord of Huelgoat's tower, made entirely of oak planks, was square and stood three storeys tall.

'I shall tell you everything,' Broérec said, 'but first you must get to know this château as well as I do. Come.'

Galeran nodded, and followed the giant into a vast hall that served as kitchen, storeroom, and, in times of war, as a stable. On one side stood an oven, with smoke escaping through a narrow slit. Flies swarmed around game that hung from the blackened beams of the ceiling. Bales of hay and bundles of firewood were piled in a corner. Near them was a trapdoor that led to a cellar, and when Broérec raised it Galeran heard a scraping noise from below.

'Go on,' said Broérec, as he placed a ladder by the door. 'You must see everything.'

The knight climbed nimbly down the wooden rungs. The cellar was deep and larger than the room above, a great storehouse for earthenware jars full of grain, barrels and salting tubs. A torch hanging from the wall gave out a smoky light. At the far end a large millstone turned slowly, driven by a man chained like a beast of burden.

'What is this?' asked Galeran.

'A millstone, my friend,' replied the blond giant with a smile.

'You haven't changed, have you, Broérec? What has this man done to deserve this?'

'Let us say that he betrayed me.'

'Like the old man I saw hanging outside?'

'No. That one stole from me.'

'What could he have stolen that was worth his life?'

'Bread,' said Broérec coldly. 'Is that a sufficient explanation for you?'

'I see,' said Galeran. 'Let us carry on with the visit. I find the air in your cellar disagreeable.'

The two men returned to the kitchen and then climbed another ladder to the first floor of the tower.

'As you can see, this is where I have my living quarters,' said Broérec. 'There are two bedrooms on this floor. I thought you would not want to share my cot so I had a bed set up in the second room.'

He pointed to a tiny room whose only light filtered in through a loophole. On a stool next to the truckle bed were a ewer filled with water, a towel of threadbare linen and a bowl.

'You thought correctly,' said Galeran as he surveyed the little room. 'The truckle bed will suit me perfectly.'

The larger bedroom was furnished with a huge box bed with sliding doors, a long table surrounded by stools, a chest that served as a wardrobe and two large benches. Drapes of red wool covered the walls, muffling sounds from outside and protecting the room from draughts.

It was September but the room was icy. Galeran wondered what it must be like in the harsh months of winter in this isolated, windswept tower. There was no fireplace to provide heat and comfort, only a large brazier that sat in the middle of the room. The knight held his hands above the glowing embers to warm the joints that were stiff after his long ride.

A loophole high up on the wall provided the little light there was during the day. The torches that were lit as soon as night fell stood ready in iron cones nailed to the wall. The only decorations in this spartan interior were banners that hung from the beams in the ceiling and an array of maces, lances and swords that took up an entire wall.

Galeran cast an expert eye over the hilts and the blades sheathed in leather.

'Let us continue,' said Broérec. 'Follow me.'

They climbed up to the next floor.

'Here there are three rooms. Two for my sons, who I may tell you do not get along, and the third is a dormitory for my men-at-arms,' he said, pointing into a room where bedding was laid out on the ground. 'The men take it in turns to sleep here. Some sleep in the cottages or in the stables. The others keep watch.'

'I didn't know you had sons.'

'Drogon and Jestin. You'll meet them soon enough. They're out hunting with some of the men, but it's getting dark so they won't be long. This is the last ladder. Up we go.'

Galeran followed him up to the top of the tower, where a flag fluttered on its wooden pole. Two men-at-arms jumped to their feet when they saw Broérec, who regarded them harshly.

High crenels topped this last storey. Above them a shelter made of wooden planks and animal skins protected the watchmen from the wind and rain.

Galeran leaned out over the crenels. The sun was sinking over the horizon, its last rays reddening the crests of the hills of Arez. The tower seemed to float like a Viking ship over the green sea of Huelgoat. It soared over the landscape, and on a clear day provided a view that stretched as far as the distant Montagne Noire, the Ar Menez Reûn Dû. A thin plume of smoke rose hesitantly above the trees a few leagues from the mountain.

'You have neighbours?' asked Galeran.

'No. People don't stay long in that part of the forest. If you get lost there you'll be found the next morning with your neck twisted and your throat slit. The old folks say that Ankou does his cooking in the rocks there and it's better not to disturb him at his work. They say death doesn't like to be watched! But it's true that the place is infested with wolves. It's probably poachers who've lit a fire there. We'll catch them when they move back onto the paths or the Carhaix road. Do you see that thing shining over there?'

'What is it? A lake?'

'Nay, it is the Yeûn and its peat bogs. An interesting place, as you'll find out.'

26

Broérec said this in such an odd tone of voice that Galeran turned to look at him. There was a strange light in the giant's eyes.

'Very well,' said Galeran, placing his hand on the man's shoulder. 'Now I have seen your château it is time for you to tell me what you want of me.'

'Let us go to my room.'

5

Broérec sent for a jug of mead and two goblets. He served Galeran a generous measure and then sat down next to him on one of the long rickety benches. He seemed lost in his thoughts, a line of worry creasing his brow. He slowly drank his cup dry and turned to look the knight in the eye. Galeran held his gaze as he savoured the honeyed drink.

'Do you remember the battles where we fought side by side, Galeran?' said Broérec.

'How could I forget?'

'What you endured for one year, I had to live through for ten. Ten years of bloody combat, ten years of knights dying for a pathetic little duke who doesn't even deserve his title!'

Broérec had turned pale, his eyes burned savagely, and beads of sweat formed at the roots of his blond hair.

'I have heard tell of this,' said Galeran. 'How did you finally manage to get away?'

'Tanguy, the Vicomte de Poher, paid part of my ransom, and my sons borrowed to pay the rest. If they had not I would still be languishing in the dungeons of Vitré, which has been the fate of many of my companions.'

'I can understand your bitterness, Broérec. But it was not to speak of this that you sent for me. How can I be of service to you?'

'Since you so badly want to know, I shall show you. Come.'

He went towards the bed.

'Have you perhaps forgotten our old Breton customs, Galeran?' he asked. 'Did you not notice something unusual when you walked into this room?'

The knight looked around him and saw that a candle burned on the table, a second near the brazier, and a third by the bed. The three candles of death were in place.

As Broérec pushed back the panels of the bed, Galeran knew he would see a body, but he did not expect it to be that of a little girl.

'This is the reason,' said Broérec. 'Or, I should say, one of the reasons. I want you to find the person who killed her.'

The body was wrapped in a shroud, and only the pale face could be seen, its eyes rolled upwards. The girl could not have been older than ten.

'Some peasants found her in the wood this afternoon. They brought her here and asked me to see that justice was done. This is the seventh body of a child that has been found in the past few months.'

The giant fell silent for a moment.

'I needn't bother to tell you', he finally went on, 'that I have never been much loved in these parts. But this business is certainly not helping matters. The peasants are rising up against me. Some of them complain that I cannot protect them from the killer, and they no longer respect or fear me. Others say I am the one who is murdering the children. As you have seen, I am practically living in a state of siege. You know me, Galeran, and you know my soul is not a gentle one, but I am not given to killing children!'

A smile crossed Galeran's lips for the first time since he had arrived at the château.

'Yes, Broérec,' he said. 'I know you are not gifted at winning people's affection. But I also know that it is not in your character to kill a child. What exactly do you expect of me?'

'You must prove my innocence, Galeran. Even here in the heart of our beloved Brittany I have heard of your exploits at the court of Louis VII. It is even said that Queen Aliénor has a certain fondness for you.'

Galeran shrugged his shoulders.

'I know that your services are much sought after,' Broérec continued. 'Even Vicomte Tanguy, who is not a man of the court, has heard tell of you. And I myself recall that it was you who found the guilty party in that sordid tale of betrayal

29

at Vitré. I want you to help me, Galeran. And that is is request you cannot refuse me,' he said in a tone of voice that brooked no reply.

'It is not courteous of you to remind me, of my obligation. My honour does not let me forget. Listen to me, Broérec, and listen well. I will help you, but if I find that it is indeed you who killed these children, I shall not rest until the point of my sword has pierced your heart.'

They looked each other up and down for a moment.

'Very well,' said Broérec, running his fingers over the scar on his cheek. 'But do you think I fear you?'

'No,' said Galeran abruptly. 'Now, tell me how this girl, and the others, met their deaths.'

'No one knows.'

'What do you mean?'

'None of the bodies showed any injuries that could have been fatal.'

The knight frowned.

'May I examine the girl? Close the door, and light a torch. I can't see a thing here.'

Broérec took one of the torches and lit it from the brazier before hanging it on the wall near the bed. Galeran leaned over the child and gently moved aside the cloth that covered the thin body with its ragged smock and breeches.

'Do you know her?' he asked.

'No. I am told she is from Lannédern.'

'But it is at least three leagues from here to Lannédern.'

'How do you know that? Hah, you must have studied the maps before setting out! Thinking ahead, as ever.'

'What was she doing so far from home?' asked Galeran, ignoring Broérec's sarcasm. 'Light another torch, I still cannot see properly.'

'I don't know what she was doing in my woods and it matters little to me. I simply wish that she had gone to die elsewhere.'

30

Broérec held the second torch while Galeran examined the girl's stiffened body.

'Give me your dagger,' the knight said. 'I need to cut open her clothes.'

He tore open the smock and the breeches, both of which bore vomit stains. Her wrists and ankles were marked with numerous blue bruises. The little hands were full of earth, the nails broken, the knees calloused.

The blade was thin enough to insert in the girl's mouth and prise open the jaw that was set in a horrible rictus. Finding nothing remarkable at the back of the mouth, he lifted up the lips and examined the teeth. A dark blue line ran along the edge of the gums.

Galeran frowned, lifted the girl by the shoulders and turned her over. Her back was covered in scars.

'By God, whoever killed her didn't do things by halves!' exclaimed Broérec, leaning over the body next to Galeran. 'Do you think it was this beating that did it?'

Galeran shook his head and stepped back a little, clearly deep in thought. He made the sign of the cross as he closed the girl's eyes, and covered the body once again with the shroud, which he knotted at both the head and the feet.

'She should be buried as soon as possible,' he said wearily. 'We must take her to Lannédern tomorrow. I want to speak with her family. Did the people who brought her here say who her parents were?'

'They said she was the inkeepers' youngest daughter.'

'Very well then. Tomorrow we shall bring them their daughter so that she may be buried on consecrated ground.'

'You realise,' said Broérec, 'that if I go there, especially with the body of yet another murdered child, I risk getting torn to pieces?'

'Do *you* realise,' snapped Galeran, 'that if you do not go you will have no hope of getting to the bottom of this mystery? Do you really think that going to ground like a hunted animal and putting the whole region to fire and sword is going to prove your innocence?'

The Lord of Huelgoat turned white with rage.

'I have not gone to ground! By God, if anyone else but you had said that to me . . .'

'Your threats do not impress me, Broérec. If you want me to help you then we must find out what is going on.'

'So be it,' said the giant, through gritted teeth. 'We shall go together to Lannédern. But I will not have you speak to me again in such a manner.'

From outside came the sound of a horn and of dogs barking, and the trumpets of the men in the watchtower sounded in response. Broérec went to the window and looked down at the men-at-arms bustling about in the courtyard.

'My sons are coming back from the hunt. We shall have boar or venison for dinner. Come, Galeran, let us join them. To show you that I bear no grudge, I shall take you on a hunt one of these days. There is no forest to match this one in the whole kingdom.'

There was fire in his voice, and Galeran remembered the man's immoderate enthusiasm for hunting. In Vitré he would abandon his post to disappear for days on the trail of some prey.

'I shall have my men put the girl in the cellar for the night. It is cool there, and I'll set someone to watch over her till morning.'

Galeran followed him down the ladder that led to the foot of the tower.

6

Torches lit the courtyard, where the stable boys were busy with the whinnying horses back from the hunt. Two huge mastiffs, hackles raised and fangs bared, growled at Galeran and advanced towards him, ready to spring.

The knight recalled the stories he had heard of dogs of war that would rip open a horse's throat before attacking the rider. He drew his sword. But then came a short whistle from a very tall young man with a torch in his hand. The dogs turned immediately and ran whimpering to their master, who received them with a kick.

Paying no attention to Galeran, the man bowed to Broérec.

'Greetings, Father. Forgive me, but a stubborn old devil led us a merry dance.'

He did not have his father's good looks, but he did have his stature. His unruly long hair and the sweat on his brow told of the ardour of the hunt. His tunic was stained, and tucked in his belt was a small oak branch, covered in blood.

'I see you got him in the end,' said Broérec, looking at the bloody branch.

The young man showed his teeth in a grin and his eyes flashed with pride.

'We did. Look, Father.'

He gave a sign, and two men-at-arms carried over a long pole from which an enormous wild boar hung by its legs. They placed the beast on the ground in front of Broérec; it was covered in wounds, its throat had been ripped open by the dogs, and an oak branch had been thrust in its mouth.

Broérec studied the beast for a moment, then slapped his son proudly on the shoulder.

'A nice catch, Drogon. He can't have been easy prey!'

Then he turned to the soldiers.

'Right, get this to the kitchens and hang it up out of the reach of these dogs from Hell!'

The men, exhausted by the day's chase, bowed to Drogon and Broérec, picked up the pole and headed off towards the keep.

'My son, this is Galeran de Lesneven, the old comrade-in-arms of whom I have spoken. We met at Vitré, almost ten years ago. Galeran, this is my eldest, Drogon.'

The two men nodded in greeting.

'Where is your brother?' asked Broérec.

'You know how he is. He disappeared at the start of the hunt. But Thustan says he's already back. He's in the stables seeing to his horse.'

'I'm not, my dear brother,' came a voice. 'I am here.'

The voice was gentle, if a little high-pitched. The young man who came forward did not look a bit like Drogon. He was around fourteen years old and still beardless. Only a light down shaded his fine lips. Small, and with black hair cut short, the boy was as slender as his brother was broad. He was dressed simply in a white tunic and dark breeches, and across is shoulder was slung a bow.

He greeted his father, then bowed to Galeran as though to mock him.

'Good day, sir. I am Jestin de Huelgoat. Thustan tells me you met Hoël in the forest on your way here.'

'What!' exclaimed Broérec. 'And you said nothing of this to me?'

'How should I know it would interest you?' retorted Galeran. 'Besides, we have not had much time to chat since I arrived. But I must say I was impressed by the chap's audacity. He claims to be the Lord of Huelgoat!'

They had reached the keep by now and climbed the ladder to the first floor. There they came upon two servants who were about to carry the body of the dead girl to the cellar.

'Who is it, Father?' asked Drogon.

'Another child. A girl.'

Jestin stood back to let the men pass.

'Do we know her?'

'Not unless you frequent the tavern in Lannédern.'

'The innkeepers' girl?'

'You do know her?' asked Galeran.

'Well, yes. I often go to Lannédern, and have even met the girl. Drogon goes there too. He's sniffing around the inkeepers' eldest daughter.'

'Hold your tongue, imbecile! I've no interest in that hussy – she's filthy and ugly. And what would a virgin like you know about women, anyway?' said Drogon with a loud laugh.

Jestin turned pale and reached for his dagger.

'One day I'll stick that in your throat.'

'That's enough!' shouted Broérec. 'Drogon, light the torches and go and check on the watch. Tell old Cléophas to get the table ready and bring us something to drink. My throat is dry with all this talking.'

Galeran looked at the two boys and marvelled at how different they were. One was as slim and graceful as the other was rugged and aggressive. But when he recalled the hatred that had blazed in Jestin's eye he wondered which of the two was the more dangerous.

Drogon lit another torch and climbed up to bark orders at the watchmen at the top of the tower. Broérec paced nervously up and down the room.

'That Hoël is no more than a peasant's bastard! He thinks he's someone just because I got his mother pregnant one day when my wife was big with child and couldn't have me. I've never understood why she didn't just enjoy it instead of running around telling everyone I raped her. I even offered to take her into the château as a servant. But she refused, her parents threw her out when Hoël was born, and she lived like a wild thing in a cave in the forest. She hanged herself when the boy was twelve. And believe it or not, Hoël dragged her body here and accused me of killing her! He swore vengeance and since then has not stopped plaguing us. At the start he

35

was too young to do us any real harm. But he grew clever as he got older, and he is a damned good archer now. But one day, Drogon or I, we'll catch the devil, and when we do . . .'

The smile on his face left no doubt as to his plans for Hoël.

'I see,' said Galeran, noting that Jestin's face had darkened during Broérec's tirade.

The boy apparently did not share their disdain for Hoël. He remained silent, his clenched fists resting on his knees.

'And your wife, Broérec?' asked Galeran. 'Have you sent her away because of your dispute with the peasants? You spoke about her all the time when we were in Vitré.'

'My wife died a long time ago,' murmured Broérec.

It was the first time Galeran had ever heard sorrow in the man's voice. He remembered how Broérec had so often praised the woman's beauty, how he had set his comrades dreaming with his descriptions of her most intimate charms.

His wife was of Germanic origin, and he had loved her with a burning passion. She was like a blonde goddess, and her skin was of a whiteness that made the moon seem dark. More than once had he left Vitré, risking charges of treachery, to ride home to visit his beloved. He would have sold his soul to be able to gaze into her cool green eyes.

'I am sorry to hear that,' said Galeran.

'It is nothing,' Broérec said gruffly. 'She gave me two fine sons. Jestin looks a lot like her . . . That's probably why I prefer him to his brother, even if he does not have Drogon's fire. He has the same eyes.'

Jestin sat fidgeting on his chair.

'May I leave, Father? I need to see the smith. I broke an arrowhead this morning. And he should have fixed your axe by now.'

'Go, my son.'

'If I may, I will go with Jestin,' said Galeran. 'I need to stretch my legs.'

Broérec made no objection. He sat there, eyes closed, fists

36

clenched, lost in thought, perhaps seeing again his lost wife's lovely face.

'What do you make of all this, Jestin?' asked Galeran, when they reached the courtyard.

The boy turned to him and spoke in a voice raw with emotion.

'What I think is that I don't much like what is going on here, sir. I'm glad you have come to help my father. There have been too many deaths already.'

'Jestin, your father told me that the bodies of five or six children have been found. Did you see them?'

'Yes, I saw some of them. But what my father did not tell you – but perhaps he doesn't know – apart from the bodies, there have been many disappearances.'

'Disappearances?'

'Twenty children in all. All around the same age, not more than fifteen years old. A monk from Braspartz told me. So it is not just here at Huelgoat.'

His voice had grown shriller as he spoke. He suddenly became aware of this and fell silent.

Galeran placed his hand on his shoulder and felt him tremble.

'We shall solve this mystery, Jestin. But I need help. Will you be my ally?'

Jestin nodded.

'Beware of Drogon, knight,' he whispered. 'He is dangerous.'

With these words the boy turned on his heels and ran off.

Galeran, perplexed, looked around for a moment before deciding to go to the stables. They were deserted, and the hayracks were almost empty. A loud whinny hailed the knight: Quolibet had recognised his master. Galeran took a fork and deposited a large helping of hay in front of the horse.

'Here you are, my friend. And you're still covered in sweat.

I'll rub you down a little. This place is most unwelcoming to us both!'

He heard a cracking sound, but when he turned he saw no one in the semi-darkness of the stable, where the horses' eyes shone with the reflected torchlight. He carried on smoothing his mount's coat. He had just finished when he heard footsteps and the door was flung open.

'My father has sent me for you. The meal is ready, sir.'

Drogon was trying to be courteous, but Galeran could tell it was not something he was used to. The fellow still seemed angry, presumably after his row with Jestin.

'Thank you, Drogon. Tell your father I am on my way.'

7

The brazier crackled with peat and heather, sending out little showers of sparks. Bowls and goblets lined the long oak table. Every torch in the room had been lit, chasing away the shadows.

Broérec was already at table. He motioned to Galeran to sit opposite him. There were a dozen or so empty stools around the table. The knight looked at them and saw just how solitary a life his host led. He took his seat, and Drogon sat clumsily next to him. Jestin quietly took his place at the end of the table, and sat as though he were a thousand leagues from his fellow diners.

'Peace be with you, Galeran,' said Broérec. 'Eat.'

He took the goblets and into them poured a thick yellowish liquid that resembled nothing more than urine.

'This is a man's drink!' he said, filling his own cup and drinking it back in one draught.

'You don't drink wine?' asked Galeran.

'No, but if you want I can open up a barrel. In the meantime, have a swig of this.'

'What is it? Barley beer?'

'No. This is a drink for birds of the night. An eau-de-vie the old cook makes from apples. He puts a bit of absinthe in there too, just to spice it up a little.'

'Absinthe!'

'So?'

'You can lose your mind on absinthe. Very well, I'll try it.'

He took a sip, and felt his tongue burn before he could swallow it.

'Clearly I am not a proper man!' he said, his eyes clouded with tears.

Broérec burst into laughter, then grabbed Galeran's goblet and downed it in one go.

'I had forgotten what it was to laugh! Ah, your wine has arrived. It's from the hills of the Loire.'

An old servant, who told Galeran his name was Cléophas, handed him a glass. The wine was cool, and a little bitter, but to him it was delicious.

Cléophas, aided by a dirty urchin who answered to the name of Titik, brought in roast game dripping with rancid fat, along with a badly cooked broth in which to dip the meat. Drogon grabbed a haunch of venison and began tearing into it with his teeth. Grease and dark blood trickled through his beard and onto his tunic.

Jestin took a pancake filled with onions and began eating silently. Cléophas had placed a jug of water in front of him.

As the meal progressed, Galeran noticed that his host ate little but drank more than was reasonable. The fetid smell of the meat brought a knot to the knight's stomach.

'Cléophas,' said Broérec, noting his lack of appetite, 'is not quite as good a cook as his wife, I have to admit. But you won't ever see her at the château. She lives near the hamlet. You'll meet none of that evil breed here, those creatures who beget bad thoughts in us, those daughters of Eve who bring only curses. Life without women, my friend, is life in paradise!'

'By my beard,' said Galeran, 'you have changed!'

'Come now, do you really think it is a loss to be deprived of the company of females? Do we not gain more than we lose? I know a thousand examples of friendship between men, but can you show me two women who are true friends?'

'I cannot disagree,' laughed Galeran. 'Women are often conceited. What they seek is not to be loved, but to be loved more than the others. They wish not to be beautiful but to be the most beautiful. But in that we are like them, for do we not also want not just to be strong, but to be the strongest? We each seek to conquer with the arms we are given. Is that a reason to hate women, particularly for you who so loved your own fair lady?'

Broérec's face became grave.

'Just a short time ago I would have killed any man who even uttered her name. But now I want to hear you speak of her again! It is true that she was all women for me, and after her I wanted none other. The truth is, I loved once and will not love again.'

He stood up, and marched up and down the room before turning to the table and standing by Galeran.

'By God, I am a happy man that I am not the father of a woman!'

Galeran was no longer listening. He had realised that Broérec's speech had a hidden meaning, but could not fathom what it was. Was he speaking of love, or of some unexpiated hatred towards womankind?

'No more of that,' said the giant suddenly. 'Can you tell me how the girl we found died? You cannot? So, even you, with your reputation, do not understand.'

Galeran's blue eyes looked at the Lord of Huelgoat, and he smiled.

'Come, answer me!' said the giant.

'You are right, Broérec, I do not know. I have just arrived here, but . . .'

'But what?' snapped Broérec.

'I think I can guess what killed the poor girl. Can you please ask your servants to leave us?'

Broérec frowned, and gave a sign to Cléophas and the boy. Then he walked over and kicked the trapdoor shut.

'Now you may speak,' he said, sitting down opposite the knight.

'I would bet that the child disappeared from Lannédern

some time ago. The marks on her wrists and ankles show she had been held prisoner. Her abductor whipped her, but that it not what caused her death.'

Galeran paused, his gaze fixed on his host. No one spoke as Broérec and his two sons waited for his next words.

'The girl had been made to work, and it was not work at the tavern. Her hands were scratched, her nails broken and full of earth. And judging from the state of her knees, I would say she had been crawling around on all fours. Finally, and here I think I am not mistaken, I would say she died from poison. That would explain the vomit. And there were other signs to suggest it.'

Broérec thumped the piece of meat he was chewing violently down on the table. Even Drogon stopped eating to stare wide-eyed at the knight. Jestin, for his part, quietly watched Galeran with his pale eyes. A silence hung over the room. Then Broérec wiped his hands on his tunic, stood up and began pacing up and down the room like a caged bear, muttering to himself.

Galeran watched him, a half-smile on his lips.

'You are still as crafty!' growled Broérec. 'Probably even more so now than when I met you. Very well, together we'll find who did this. And I shall not be ungrateful.'

'All I seek is to be freed from my debt.'

'You will be cleared of your obligation. That I swear to you in front of my sons.'

He turned to the two young men.

'Leave us, I want to be alone with my friend.'

They saluted their father and left the room.

'We shall be together for some time,' Broérec said to Galeran, 'so let us speak frankly. I know that you have detested me ever since the incident with the girl in Vitré.'

Galeran clenched his jaw but said nothing.

'I do not want to have to watch out for any mischief from you,' said the giant. 'You are a man of honour. Let me explain what happened.'

42

'There is nothing to explain,' said Galeran drily, getting to his feet. 'Besides, ten years have gone by. I do not love you, but it matters little. You saved my life once, and now I shall repay you and never see you again.'

His voice lacked any intonation.

'Listen,' said Broérec, who appeared not to have been listening. 'It was not I who killed her. When you captured her, you will remember, the provost decided to throw her into the dungeon until he made his judgement. Some of the men said she was Robert de Vitré's mistress, and so she was condemned for treason against the Duke of Cornwall. But the truth is that she was just too beautiful! And that the murder you hate me for was not carried out by my hand. After our duel and your departure for Lesneven, I found the men responsible and hanged them.'

Galeran stood at the brazier, rubbing his hands over the embers. He could feel anger rising up within him, his pulse beating in his temples.

'I had drunk too much,' said Broérec, who seemed overcome by an urge to confess. 'That much is true. But when I left her she was still alive and, by my faith, still a virgin. I wanted to ask for her forgiveness and make her my mistress, for she pleased me as much as she pleased you. I did not wish to possess her in that stinking, rat-infested hole. But after I'd gone some of the men went there and ravished her. She managed to grab one of their daggers. When you found her there the next morning, her clothes torn from her body and a knife planted in her chest . . .'

'Enough, Broérec,' said Galeran in a voice ice-cold with anger.

The giant fell silent. The conflict was out in the open again. The conflict that, ten years earlier, had pitted them one against the other, a duel from which Galeran had emerged with his forehead indelibly marked by the curved blade of Broérec's scimitar.

'Let us call a truce until you have solved the mystery of

these deaths,' said Broérec. 'Then we can fight if you still wish to. But do not forget that I do not fear you.'

He opened the door of the tiny room where Galeran was to sleep.

'Wait, I'll give you something to cover yourself with.'

He went to his own bed and picked up a thick fur.

'You'll need this. The tower is cold as the grave at night.'

He turned and left the room, leaving the door open behind him. Galeran threw the fur over his bed.

Suddenly a familiar whistling sound jolted Broérec as the knight's dagger hurtled past his ear to pierce the wooden frame of his bed.

'If I thought you had killed her,' Galeran said slowly and calmly, 'one of us would be dead by now. But I heard what you did after I left for Lesneven. I knew you were innocent. Sleep peacefully, for I have never killed a man whose back was to me.'

Broérec removed the knife and placed it on the table. He took off his boots, climbed into bed fully clothed and closed the shutters behind him.

Galeran, a smile on his lips, went over to the table to get his knife and then retired to his room, closing the door behind him. He suddenly felt exhausted, and the cold made him shiver. He placed his weapons at arm's length and got into bed. He too kept his clothes on.

He could not sleep. The day had been too full of brutal contrasts for his mind to rest. That morning he had left the tranquillity of his family home, a house governed by a man of wisdom and equity. Now he was in an infernal place ruled by madness and despair.

Anger and pity battled in the knight's heart as a host of images flashed through his mind: the old man on the gallows, the fellow turning the millstone like a beast of burden, Hoël the bastard emerging from the undergrowth to proclaim his rights and his hatred, the ghastly face and battered body of the girl whose death cried out for vengeance . . .

The sound of footsteps and barked orders signalled the changing of the guard. It was around midnight, and Galeran was just beginning to doze off, when he heard the neighing of a horse. He thought of Quolibet, and rushed to the loop-hole to look out. At first he could see nothing in the darkness, but then he began to make out the silhouettes of two horses standing saddled in the yard. A giant of a man was heaving himself up on one of the beasts. The man was Broérec, and the man at his side looked like the sinister Thustan. The pair disappeared over the drawbridge.

Galeran went back to his bed. Despite his continuing unease, he managed to fall into a deep sleep. But as he slipped into unconsciousness a phrase echoed round his head: 'This is a drink for birds of the night! A drink for birds of the night. Birds of the night . . .'

PART TWO

PART TWO

Kentoc'h mervel eget mastared.
(It is better to die than to be tainted.)

Breton motto

8

People did not like to venture into this part of the Bois-Haut for, it was said, fairies still lived here. Perhaps it was because everything seemed more luminous here, from the tops of the trees to the bright green moss on the ground. Columns of light, rays from the sun or the moon, pierced through to the long grass and the undergrowth. In autumn the leaves turned later in this part of the forest. Blocks of lichen-covered granite rose between the conifers. Waves of ferns green as unripe almonds swept along the trunks damp with sap.

She walked silently, her bare feet hardly touching the ground. Above her, the wind lashed the tops of the pine trees. Dressed in dark breeches and a white smock tied at the waist with a thin linen cord, the girl had the supple grace of a fawn.

Adjusting the heavy gamebag and the bow she carried on her shoulder, she climbed up a mass of fallen rocks. Once at the top she aimed for the steep cliff to one side of the summit. A dull rumble shook the ground around her. She ignored it, crouched down, and, moving aside the lower branches of an ash tree that grew on the rock, disappeared through a narrow crevice.

She crawled for some time along a tunnel cut by rainwater before coming to a small lake hidden from the world by high walls of granite. This was her refuge, and in all the time she had been coming here she had found no other entrance to it.

The young man who had followed her all morning lay on the ground and waited after he saw her disappear into the hill. He cautiously approached the place where she had vanished, discovered the crevice and, without hesitation, slid inside.

He was astounded by the sight that met his eyes when he

reached the end of the tunnel. The lake was like an emerald set in a crown of granite, its centre pierced by the white arrow of a cascade. A pebble beach rose gently from the water. Ferns grew up the sides of the granite walls. Fish leaped from the water and dragonflies brushed the surface with their diaphanous wings.

The man, tall and very blond, watched the girl and saw that here, isolated from the world of men, she was at home.

She went into a little cave on the side of the cliff. He crawled silently along a ridge and hid in a crevice near the entrance to the cave, whose floor was covered in fine white sand. An old blanket lay at the back, neatly folded over a bed of straw. A large flat stone served as a table and a log as a seat.

The girl placed her gamebag on the stone. Then, despite the chill in the air, she began to undress, casting her breeches and smock onto the bed. She undid the strips of cloth that held her breasts in place and began to slowly massage her chest. Entirely naked now, she ruffled her hair with her hand and stretched voluptuously. Here, at least she felt free.

She strode out of the cave, kicking the sand with her feet, and went down to the pebble beach. After a brief glance around her, she entered the water, gasping as the cold gripped her body. She walked slowly at first, then suddenly dived under and swam towards the cascade.

The young man, stupefied by desire, watched the slender silhouette glide through the lake. The water was so clear that the sandy bottom was visible. Silvery trout flashed by the naked swimmer's body.

She stopped by the waterfall to let the tumbling water gush over her breasts and hips, and stayed there a long moment before swimming back to the shore and running to the cave to dry herself vigorously with a piece of cloth.

When she had dressed she went to the back of the cave and moved aside some branches that covered a small pit. From this she took a cloth bag. She sat on her bed and held the bag upside down to let its contents fall pell-mell onto the blanket.

It contained a small mirror made of polished pewter and a chain at the end of which hung a pretty locket of finely wrought silver.

She wiped the mirror with the back of her hand and examined her reflection, passing her hand through her short hair and biting her lips to make them as red as cherries. Then she took the silver locket and opened it. A lock of blond hair fell to the ground. She took it in her hands and gently kissed it, her eyes half closed.

She put her treasures back in the bag and stored it in the pit, which she carefully covered with dead leaves. She was radiant now.

Opening her gamebag, she took a white cloth which she placed over the table. She filled a goblet with water from the lake and put it on the table along with a cob loaf and three knives. Eagerly she placed a coin beside the bread and spoke in a voice that quivered with excitement.

'I honour thee, fairies. Protect me from hatred. Give me strength and wisdom. Wine I shall offer you the next time.'

Thus the fairies accorded her help and support in the ordeals she was to face.

It was this moment that the young man chose to make his entrance. His bulk cast an inordinately large shadow across the clear sand. The girl started, her eyes wide with fright. She recognised him, and clenched her fists as she sat down again at the table.

'Don't be afraid,' said the young giant in a muffled voice.

'Come no closer, or by my faith, I shall kill you!' cried the girl, seizing one of the knives.

'You know who I am. We played together as children.'

'How did you find me?' she asked coldly.

'I've seen you wandering about before dawn. So for once I decided to follow you.'

He paused to look more closely at her face and her slender figure.

'I did not expect this. I really did not. You are cunning, you

51

play your game very well. I must have been blind all these years!'

'Well then, go on being blind and go away!' she replied forcefully, a savage light in her pale eyes.

The young man looked admiringly around him and went on as though he had not heard her.

'This lake is like a little paradise. And the cave you have made into your shelter. And you!'

'Do you hear me? Go away!' she screamed.

'Do you forget who I am?' he asked. 'We go back a long way, and you know it.'

'Nonsense! Go, and forget me and forget this place.'

'No,' he replied calmly, appearing not to notice the knife she brandished.

Then he suddenly leapt forward and grabbed her arm, twisting it behind her and opening her fingers one by one until she dropped the weapon. She cried out in pain and bit his finger, but he lifted her as he would a child and carried her to the back of the cave.

'Let me go!' she shouted. 'You will pay for this!'

'I'll let you go when you have calmed down.'

He flung her onto the bed, still gripping her with one hand.

'Now, listen to me,' he said. 'You are no better than I am. Père Gwen taught me the Holy Scriptures. There it is written that we are all the same before God. You have forgotten that, and now you know only how to give orders. You were not like that when you were a child.'

His voice had changed, had become angry. The girl sensed this and stopped resisting, her breath coming rapidly.

'What is your real name?' he asked.

She gave no response.

'Tell me,' he insisted. 'There is no point hiding it now.'

'Ninian,' she blurted out.

9

The brazier had gone cold and the first rays of light were filtering in through the narrow slit of the loophole. Galeran, who had finally managed to fall asleep in the early hours, threw off the thick fur that covered his body and put on his boots. His head was a little sore, the ache a reminder of the Loire wine and the strange liqueur of the night before.

A horn sounded three times. He heard a commotion above his head in the men-at-arms' dormitory. He put on his coat of mail and his tunic, slipped a bowl into his bag and went out of the bedroom. He smiled at the loud snores emerging from Broérec's bed.

'The night bird has returned to its nest!'

He walked quietly across the room and climbed down the ladder to the floor below.

Cléophas, his face running with sweat, his thinning grey hair tied with a dirty piece of cloth, was already busy at his ovens making buckwheat pancakes. Galeran's stomach turned when he smelled the familiar odour of rancid oil that filled the room.

A manservant slept on a straw bed next to the trapdoor that led to the cellar. His mouth yawned open as he groaned in his sleep, dribbling saliva slowly down his cheek. Cléophas' ragged assistant stretched as he sat up on the pile of hay that had been his bed.

The carcass of the boar that had been the main dish of the previous evening's meal hung from a hook in the ceiling, swinging gently to and fro as bluebottles swarmed around the bloody cuts in its flesh. One of Drogon's dogs sat on the ground below the dead beast, its snout raised. It growled when Galeran entered the room but did not move.

The knight greeted Cléophas cordially before going to the

hearth to fill his bowl with warm ashes. Cléophas turned to him, unused to being addressed in a tone that was neither hostile nor insulting. He opened his toothless mouth as though to speak, but no words came out. The old man had not spoken in such a long time that he had almost forgotten how. Yet there were so many things he could tell . . .

Galeran went out into the courtyard to stretch his numbed limbs. His neck was sore and his muscles ached after the night in the freezing bedroom. There were a few clouds in the sky, but the day promised to be fine. Crows circled slowly above the keep. His headache was easing and he began to feel generally better here in the bracing air. He went through the first enclosure into the lower courtyard, humming an old ballad as he walked.

The servants and the men-at-arms were attending to the dozen or so horses that stamped their feet impatiently in the stables. When he reached the cistern Galeran placed his bowl on a flat stone. He heaved off the heavy wooden cover and filled a bucket with icy water. He undressed his upper body and began vigorously rubbing his back and chest with ashes from the bowl. When he had finished, he leaned forwards to wash his face before splashing the freezing water over his torso. He dried himself with his tunic and put his clothes back on. Then he sharpened his knife on the stone and began to shave.

A sonorous laugh made him turn. Broérec, his tunic crumpled and his hair dishevelled, stood behind him.

'You haven't changed! You're the only one in the whole place who washes and shaves in the morning. That's all very well in fine weather, but at this time of year . . .'

Galeran merely smiled in response and carried on with his ablutions.

Broérec looked at him suspiciously.

'You slept well, I hope? Nothing disturbed you?'

'I slept like a log,' lied the knight. 'When do we leave for Lannédern?'

'As you can see, I told the men to have the horses ready at first light. We'll leave when we have eaten some pancakes and drunk some mead.'

'Good. But I'm not very hungry. The oil the old man is using smells as though it hasn't been changed since the Crusades! The food here is even worse than at Vitré.'

'You are right, but I have tried other cooks and they were worse.'

With that they went off to breakfast, and a short time later mounted their horses for the journey. Their little troop, led by Thustan and Drogon, rode out through the courtyard.

10

The big black dogs raced off like arrows from a bow as soon as the drawbridge was lowered. Preceded by ten soldiers bearing javelins, Galeran and Broérec rode side by side. Behind them, led by a man on foot, came a horse bearing the dead girl's body tied across a pack-saddle with a stout rope. The horses whinnied with delight, great clouds of steam streaming from their nostrils into the chilly morning air.

Galeran could sense the men's anxiety. Their pace was slow, and they gripped their javelins tightly as they looked fearfully around them.

They passed the foot of a rocky hill and rode along the outer wall of the château. Drogon gave a sign to Thustan, and the pair rode off ahead with the dogs to act as scouts. The troop soon reached the cover of the trees, where it followed a path that snaked through the forest amid violet heather and broom. Broérec told Galeran that many foxes had their nests along this track.

'I used to hunt them with my lady,' he added, and the knight saw pain in his eyes.

The riders now left the wood and arrived at the hamlet of Huelgoat. Here was more evidence of the misery of life in small Breton villages. The hamlet consisted of five little reed-thatched hovels, which lodged both humans and beasts. There was no church and no cemetery. But at the crossroads were ten cairns around a stone cross, and this place served as a burial site for those that Ankou seized. Such was Broérec's domain.

The village looked deserted, and Galeran noticed that no smoke emerged from the roofs. Even the gates to the animal enclosures lay open. The only living creature to be seen was an old dog that ran off barking as soon as the riders appeared.

56

'Shall we go in, Father?' asked Drogon, with a nod towards the largest shack.

'No, we are not here for that. You can take care of that later.'

'What is happening here?' asked the knight.

'These swinish peasants have been refusing to pay their rent and won't even perform the labour they owe me. I have made Drogon my intendant and told him to set the dogs on them if they don't pay up.'

'I see,' said Galeran. 'But didn't you have an intendant when you were in Vitré?'

'Indeed,' replied Broérec with a grin. 'It was Cléophas and that awful wife of his who looked after my fief.'

'Cléophas the cook?'

'The very same! And a scoundrel he is too!'

'He is not an honest man?'

'Oh, he was honest, all right. Maybe even too honest, in my opinion. He said I shouldn't squeeze the peasants too much, nor the serfs. Tell me, Galeran, don't you think that in a war one cannot afford to wait for money to come in? For money to pay the troops? Those miscreant mercenaries would go over to the other side if they were offered a good feast!'

'I know,' sighed the knight. 'Money is the backbone of war. It's all too common now to meet men who fight for a living and who care not a whit for or against whom they do battle. But don't you think your attitude towards your peasants is just as dangerous? Particularly when they have the means to defend their land?'

'That's just what Cléophas said,' replied Broérec. 'He spent too long listening to their moaning: "It's cold, it's hot, the cow is dead, my wife is sick . . ." And all the time I wasn't getting a penny. Believe me, Thustan and Drogon will get it out of them. As for Cléophas, he's fine where he is with his nose stuck in his atrocious soup.'

'And you, Broérec, you are no longer master of your house!' retorted the knight.

The giant did not reply. He gave a sign to his men to slow their horses down to a walk as they passed through the hamlet. But they encountered no resistance. It was as though the peasants had been warned of their visit and had taken refuge in the forest.

As soon as Huelgoat was behind them the vegetation grew dense. All around stood ferns, as high as a man, that waved gently in the wind. Around them, creatures took flight into the rotting green swamp as the troop approached. From afar came the harsh cry of a wolf. The horses whinnied nervously and champed at the bit.

'Are there many wolves in these parts?' asked Galeran.

'Yes. The cattle must be watched at all times, particularly in winter. We shall have to organise a beat with the peasants to get rid of them. Drogon lost one of his men last winter, not far from the château. The idiot went into the rocks alone and got half his face bitten off! We think it was a huge wolf that did it, but no one ever saw the beast.'

'And the dogs couldn't find its trail?'

'They did, but the wolf must have come from Hell, for they would not follow it. They lay down and whimpered, and not even a beating from Drogon could make them get up again.'

'A beast from Hell . . .' murmured Galeran.

'Hey, you over there!' roared Broérec at one of his men who had inadvertently wandered off the track. 'Get back in line.'

Galeran glanced quickly around him and instinctively put his hand to his sword. He heard the sound of something crashing through the undergrowth, then saw a squirrel running across the path chased by one of the mastiffs. Drogon, who had now returned to ride at the front of the troop, whistled, and the dog crept sheepishly back to its master.

Galeran gave himself a shake. He was angry at himself, and deeply uneasy. The atmosphere in this forest was no more agreeable to him than that of the château.

*

Thustan guided the little troop to the Elez. After crossing the dank peat bog of the Yeûn, the river ran by Saint-Herbot before disappearing into the rocks near the Aulne and joining the immense ocean that lies, according to the ancients, under Armorica.

The Elez was not very high at this time of year, and the dogs ran up and down the banks, their noses at water level as they sought out a ford. They eventually found one and flung themselves into the water, soon followed by their master and the other riders.

Once on the other side Broérec gave a sign to Galeran that he should follow him a little apart from the others. He led him in the direction of a powerful rumbling noise that came from nearby, where the river cascaded into a dark ravine.

'This is the giant Gewr's waterfall,' said Broérec, shouting to make himself heard above the din. 'They say that these rocks are all that is left of the giant's work. He was a stonecutter like his two brothers, and so tall he could step over mountains. The old folk say that when he died they had to cut him into nine pieces before they could bury him.'

Galeran smiled. Like all Bretons, as a child he had heard many such tales recounted of an evening. A sudden melancholy took hold of him, and he wondered whether it was true that in Brittany the fog was so thick that people's heads filled up with dreams.

He hastened to catch up with Broérec, who had already turned to rejoin the troop.

'Who is Herbot?' he asked. 'Another legend?'

'Not at all. He was a hermit here. They say he was very fond of animals and preferred their company to that of humans. He had two white oxen that followed him everywhere; their ghosts still wander the hills of Arez. His house has become a chapel, and the cattle often wander down there from the hillsides as though they were on a pilgrimage. The peasants hereabouts venerate him and see him as the protector of their livestock.'

The two men quickly caught up with the others, who were waiting at the entrance to the village of Saint-Herbot. The hamlet lay in a pretty valley full of beech trees. As well as the former lodgings of the holy man, there were twelve houses and a cemetery.

The village was eerily calm. Just as in Huelgoat, the doors of the shacks were barred, the windows shuttered, and there was no smoke to signal the presence of human beings. There were no old men or women sitting on the doorsteps, no children playing outside.

'And what is going on here?' asked Galeran, amazed to see yet another lifeless village. 'Where are all the peasants? You did tell me that they no longer feared you enough.'

'They go to ground like the rats that they are. They're afraid of Ankou, of me, of the dead children . . . What do I know! Come, let us leave this place.'

With that he dug his heels into his horse's side and galloped off, signalling to his escort to follow him.

11

Galeran saw plumes of smoke rising up into the clear sky as they approached Lannédern. At least this village had not been abandoned by its inhabitants.

A chapel stood in the centre of a large enclosure surrounded by a stone wall. The villagers apparently lived under God's protection, for their houses were within the consecrated enclosure. The wall, higher than was usual for such villages could be entered only by a heavy oak door that was locked at night.

As in most Breton villages, the grassy cemetery was small. Tradition demanded that the dead were regularly exhumed to make room for new arrivals. Their bones were then placed in the ossuary that was dug along the side of the enclosure.

As the troop approached the village, Galeran saw that what he had taken for houses standing outside the wall were in fact a barn, a byre, a pigsty and what was undoubtedly the famous tavern of Lannédern. The tolerance of the church did not extend to permitting this den of iniquity to lie within its walls.

Children were playing beside a muddy duckpond near the enclosure. An old woman sat on a stool making a basket, glancing up from time to time at them. Chickens foraged at her feet. A young man, his feet covered in mud, was leading some heifers out of the byre. He stopped short when he saw the horsemen and hurried back inside the outhouse.

Warned no doubt by a lookout, the villagers had gathered round the entrance to the enclosure, blocking the route. Lannédern's population consisted of no more than twenty men and as any women, a gaggle of children and a few old folk. Galeran also spotted a group of urchins who gathered around a shepherd boy and who stood a little apart from the villagers and their children.

Two men came forward to speak to the troop. The first was a thin, white-haired old man, probably the village priest, whose long strides made his chasuble billow as he walked. The second was a squat monk, his lowered hood hiding his face. His habit, black like those of the monks of Cluny, reached down to his heels.

'So you have come, my lord,' said the old man, bowing to Broérec. 'Who told you?'

'Told me what?' asked Broérec as he got down off his horse and handed the reins to one of his men-at-arms.

'About the boy they found dead yesterday by the Elez,' stuttered the priest. 'The one Renoulf and his son brought here.'

'You mean there's another one?' growled Broérec.

'You . . . you . . .'

'Stop stuttering! We have brought a dead child too. Send someone for the innkeepers, and fast!'

The old man called over one of the boys playing by the pond and whispered his orders in the child's ear.

Broérec's men, on Drogon's orders, had taken up position a short distance from the entrance to the village. They sat silently on their horses, their hands on their javelins. Only Thustan and the man holding the horses stood next to Broérec.

A murmur ran through the crowd of peasants when they saw what the packhorse was carrying. The tension between the two groups was palpable. Drogon gave a sign and his men slowly approached the entrance to the enclosure. The village women sent their small children indoors and closed the doors behind them. Then they came and stood defiantly next to their husbands.

'Broérec has told the truth about one point at least,' thought Galeran. 'These people have no love for him. When peasant women bare their teeth, as my father says, revolt is never far away.'

The group of boys he had noticed earlier were still keeping their distance from the peasants, as though they were not part of the village. There was something unusual in their attitude that aroused the knight's curiosity. The shepherd boy, who looked about fourteen, observed the doings of the horsemen and the villagers. He signalled to the boys around him to disperse, then walked with much self-assurance towards the villagers, who moved aside to let him pass. He went towards the priest, but the monk placed a firm hand on his shoulder and led him into the village.

A man-at-arms, upon an order given by Broérec, undid the rope that held the dead girl's body on the saddle and laid the corpse roughly down on the ground. An angry murmur ran through the crowd of peasants, who began inching forwards towards the Lord of Huelgoat.

A man and a woman, led by the boy the priest had sent off, made their way to the front of the rabble. The pot-bellied man bowed to Broérec.

'I am the innkeeper and this is my wife. You sent for me, my Lord?'

'Look first and then we shall talk,' Broérec replied harshly.

He took his dagger and cut open the white shroud to reveal the dead girl's deformed face. Galeran could smell a faint odour of decomposition.

The woman looked at her daughter and smothered a cry before burying her face in her hands. The innkeeper, his face deathly pale, moved her behind him.

'Who killed our little one?' he asked in a tone that mixed incredulity with rage.

'I do not know,' replied Broérec haughtily.

'One moment!' interrupted Galeran, sensing that it was best to step in now before Broérec's heartlessness turned this already fraught situation into a violent one.

'I greet you, innkeeper,' he said. 'I am Galeran de Lesneven and I would like to express my sympathy for you and your wife in your hour of trouble. We have come here to help, not to accuse. Sir Broérec and myself think it is time to put a stop to the terrible events that have been plaguing the land.'

The innkeepers, more used to the brutal manner of their lord, looked at each other in astonishment.

'We have come,' continued Galeran, 'to find out what caused the death of your girl and of the other child who has been brought here.'

He turned to the priest.

'May we go to your chapel to talk? You can bring the girl to prepare her for burial. I have already examined her. Have you buried the boy?'

The knight had imperceptibly taken control of proceedings and the old clergyman sensed this.

'No, sir,' he said, almost bowing before the knight. 'I have not yet laid him to rest. I plan to bury him today.'

He now addressed a couple of the villagers.

'You two, carry la Fanchonette into the village and sound the death knell so that others come to join the old women watching over the boy in the chapel.'

He gave a sign to the villagers to move aside and let the visitors enter the enclosure. The women began to move slowly back towards their houses as the two men chosen by the priest picked up the dead girl's body and carried it towards the chapel. Père Gwen went to open the church doors.

'Please,' he said, standing aside to let the visitors enter.

Thustan, who stuck to his master like a leech, went in after Galeran and Broérec.

The chapel was modest, but very clean. A candle burned near the altar, which was a slab of stone covered with a white cloth, and bouquets of heather decorated a niche which held a statue of the Virgin Mary. A lamp stood on each corner of the altar, and the narrow windows cast slender beams of sunlight that illuminated the pulpit, a simple wooden block upon which the priest stood to preach.

Galeran motioned to the innkeeper's wife to sit on one of the benches.

The two villagers deposited the girl's body on the earthen floor at the foot of the altar. Another shroud lay there, on which had been placed bouquets of flowers. Two old women knelt alongside to pray for the repose of the boy's soul.

The sound of the bell rang out over the village. Soon others would come to join the old women.

The innkeeper's wife seemed overcome with grief. Galeran watched her as she sat on the bench, and thought that she must once have been very beautiful, before the rigours of her life had taken their toll. Her husband stood behind her, his hands resting on her shoulders.

'Woman, you must help me find who killed your girl,' Galeran said softly. 'Tell me how and when she disappeared.'

She lifted her tear-stained eyes to him and spoke with difficulty.

'La Fanchon went missing the day the fox ate old Mikhel's chicken!'

'When was that? How many moons ago? Was it perhaps a mass day?'

'The day before mass. Yes, it was the day before.'

'So it was a Saturday. But which Saturday?'

'I don't know, sir.'

'Was it before the harvest?'

'No, after.'

'Are you sure? That would make it two months ago. And how did it happen?'

The woman began sobbing.

'I don't know, sir,' she muttered, wiping her nose with her sleeve.

'Try to remember. What did you do that Saturday? Were you at the inn? Where was Fanchon? Were there any strangers at the inn?'

'I remember the young sir was there,' she said hesitantly.

Broérec, who had been attentively following the conversation, raised his fist threateningly at the woman.

'What!' he roared. 'You dare speak of my son, strumpet?'

The woman crouched back on her bench and her husband readied himself to protect her. But Galeran took Broérec by the arm and led him aside. The giant resisted a little, but the knight's grip was so firm that he grudgingly gave in and followed him.

'Listen, Broérec, you asked me to help you, did you not?' said Galeran angrily.

'Yes, but . . .'

'Well then, let me take care of this. I can't get any information from these people if you stand there threatening them. And if one of your sons is somehow involved in this, then we must know!'

'Very well,' muttered Broérec. 'I'll be quiet. But just let these bumpkins try to put the blame on my sons!'

'If one of your sons is guilty then you must punish him. Now, please listen to what is said here but do not intervene. If you do, I shall withdraw my assistance in this matter.'

The two men returned to the waiting innkeepers.

'Now,' said Galeran, 'can you tell me which of the lord's sons was here that day?'

There was no reply.

'Don't be afraid,' said the knight. 'I give you my word that no harm will come to you. We need to know who was in Lannédern at the time, whether it was Broérec's son, a vagabond, a hunter or anyone else.'

'The blond one drank under our roof. But the other one was here too.'

'Do you mean they were both in Lannédern that Saturday?'

'Yes, they were both here.'

The innkeeper hesitated.

'The brown-haired one', he went on in a low voice, 'was in the enclosure to pray and he even played with our little one afterwards. He's not a proud one, and he's gentle. La Fanchon liked him. But the blond one . . . He's been sniffing around Armelle, our eldest, for a while now. It took a few men from the village to make him leave her alone. By God, but she was frightened of him!'

'La Fanchon was not with you in the tavern?'

'No, she was at the ossuary. But I was keeping an eye on her. And then all of a sudden, as though Ankou had taken her, she wasn't there any more!' she said, bursting into tears.

Her husband crossed himself.

'Be quiet, woman,' he said. 'Go back to the inn. I shall speak to you alone, knight. My wife has been beside herself since our daughter went missing.'

Galeran nodded in agreement.

'Thank you for your help,' he said to the woman. 'May God protect you.'

The innkeeper watched his wife walk away before continuing.

'We searched everywhere for our Fanchon,' he said with a deep sigh. 'The whole village helped, but it was in vain. And as the days passed . . .'

'Were the lord's two sons still in the village when you noticed she had gone?'

'Oh, no. The brown-haired one had taken his brother away. They argued about Armelle – he told him to stop bothering her.'

'Have any other children disappeared from this or other villages?'

'Well, Ankou has been prowling around for a long time now. And then there is the Yeûn . . .' he murmured, and his eyes seemed to see some terrible vision behind Galeran.

The knight looked around quickly, but all he could see was the priest deep in conversation with the monk near the altar. He turned back to the innkeeper. Sweat trickled down the man's face and into his eyes.

'What has made you afraid all of a sudden, innkeeper?'

'Nothing,' the man whispered. 'Nothing. It's just all these

67

things happening all at once. A girl disappears in the Yeûn, and then a boy from Huelgoat after the harvest, the same time as our Fanchon. And in Saint-Herbot Janik's two sons have disappeared . . . As I said, Ankou is on the prowl!'

Broérec had wandered off when the talk turned away from his sons, and from where he now stood he could not have heard the innkeeper's last words, for the man had spoken in so quiet a voice that Galeran had to lean forward to hear him.

The innkeeper crossed himself again. He was sweating even more profusely now and hopped from one foot to the other.

'Sit down,' said Galeran. 'Be calm. We shall find the guilty one and we shall punish him. There is no sorcery. Rest a moment and then you may return to your tavern.'

'Yes, sir,' said the innkeeper, resting his head in his hands.

The priest, who had maintained a discreet distance during the interview, now went to the distressed man and whispered some words of comfort in his ear.

Nearby, Broérec was in heated conversation with Thustan. The pair fell silent when Galeran approached them.

'Is your Latin so bad that you do not wish me to hear it?' joked Galeran. 'I shall have to speak with Jestin and Drogon, as you can imagine.'

His former comrade-in-arms gave him a strange look.

'Jestin is back at the château and you can speak with Drogon tonight,' he said. 'But not here in front of these fools.'

'As you wish. Tell me, were you aware of the disappearances on your land?'

'What disappearances? I have told you what I know. There were deaths, but everyone has to die sometime.'

'I think you are not telling me everything. You, the lord of these parts, claim to know less than a humble innkeeper. Not only have there been deaths, but there have been many more than we thought. And many people have disappeared. Whatever is going on here is more complicated than you have told me. A disappearance is often a more distressing thing than a death . . .'

'My friend, you trouble me. How can I know what is going on among these boors who run from me as though I were the Devil himself?'

'Have you not made a census of them and their livestock?'

The giant shook his head and grimaced.

'How do you think I can count people or beasts that are not there? I told you these folk are not co-operative.'

'Fear does not kill, Broérec. But watch out, for it does make it impossible to live.'

He turned on his heels and walked off before the giant could respond.

'What is to become of us, sir?' said the old priest, hurrying to catch up with Galeran.

He too was sweating, and his breath came haltingly.

'Father, will you help me solve this mystery?'

'I will do what I can. But I am just a weary old man.'

'First, Father, tell me who the monk is who was with you.'

'That is Frère Withénoc. A very holy man, sir,' he added, with a note of hesitation in his voice that did not escape Galeran's attention. 'But he is a man who does not much esteem the company of others.'

'That I had remarked. Can you introduce me to him? I should like to meet him. And . . .'

The knight stopped in mid-sentence, and his pensive face showed that an idea of some sort had come to him.

'Who was that strange boy that Frère Withénoc took into the enclosure just after we arrived?'

'That must have been Kaourintin, the shepherd. He has been visited by Our Lord . . .'

The priest fell silent. Galeran turned and saw that the monk was walking slowly towards them.

'What is it, Father?' asked Galeran. 'Are you ill?'

'It is nothing, my son. I am just an old man who grows tired very easily. Will you forgive me if I leave you now? I must pray for the souls of these two children.'

'Of course. Will you permit me to examine the boy's body?'

'Please. May God shield you,' the priest murmured, and withdrew a little too quickly.

He placed a hand on the innkeeper's shoulder as he passed and the man stood up and followed him out of the chapel. Broérec and Thustan had also gone. Now, apart from the two old women kneeling by the altar, Galeran was alone with Frère Withénoc. The monk, his hood still concealing his face, had stopped a couple of yards from the knight.

A feeling of unease once again took hold of Galeran. He could not tell if it stemmed from the thought of the two murdered children, or from the dark figure that stood before him.

He gave himself a shake and marched up to the monk.

'I am Galeran de Lesneven. And you are Frère Withénoc?'

The monk said nothing and kept his head lowered. The only feature that could be distinguished under his cowl was a fine black beard cut in the English style. A heavy silence hung between the two men. Galeran, who was growing impatient with this little game, was about to speak again when a muffled voice emerged from the monk's habit.

'I am indeed Frère Withénoc, Sir Galeran. We shall meet again. But be careful here, for this land is full of danger, especially for those who are too curious.'

With that he turned and strode out of the church.

'This devil of a monk has sent a chill up my spine!' thought Galeran.

The knight set about examining the dead boy's body. He asked the two old women kneeling by the corpse to leave him alone for a while, then moved aside the bouquets of flowers and removed the shroud. The body had been washed. Unlike the girl, the boy did not seem to have been beaten. Galeran could find no wounds. The child must have been around eight or nine years old and was excessively thin. The knight frowned as he examined his mouth. The gums were marked with the same dark line as the girl's. And once again, his nails were broken and his knees bruised.

Galeran replaced the shroud, crossed himself and left the chapel, signalling to the old women to return to their places alongside the bodies of the dead children.

12

A fine September sun shone over the village. The air was warm, and Galeran was glad to be out of the dark chapel. He felt alone and helpless. He needed an ally he could trust, but had no confidence in either Broérec or his sons, despite the fellow-feeling he had initially had for Jestin.

He left the enclosure and was heading for the inn when Broérec came to meet him.

'Have you not finished yet?' the giant said scornfully. 'I have things to do at the château and I need to talk to Jestin. I have not seen him since yesterday. I'll leave one of my men here to accompany you.'

'I have only to visit the inn and then I shall be ready to leave,' said Galeran in a weary tone that caught Broérec's attention.

'What's wrong with you that you seem so tired all of a sudden?'

'I'm fine. Where have Drogon and Thustan gone?'

'Back to Huelgoat. Drogon was fed up waiting. He's not known for his patience.'

Galeran looked at Broérec curiously.

'What are you thinking of now?'

'Of patience, my friend, of patience . . .'

Broérec shrugged his shoulders as he watched the knight walk off towards the inn. He shouted an order and his men fell into line; one of them brought him his horse. He mounted and rode off, his soldiers galloping behind him.

When the cloud of dust had settled Galeran heard the ringing of a bell. The lookout, perched on top of the chapel, was giving the sign that the alert was over and the villagers could now go back to their occupations.

Galeran watched as village life returned to normal. A pedlar had just arrived in the hamlet and was cheerfully hawking his ribbons and his bone pins. Children skipped about him and laughed at his incessant jokes and patter. Their mothers, rather more sober, quietly asked the price of a brooch or a length of yarn and haggled patiently before paying a price they were happy with.

The pedlar also served as a messenger, bringing news of relatives and friends from one village to another.

An old woman from the Yeûn had set up her hand-drawn cart near the ossuary and was selling pancakes covered in golden honey. Two little girls, hand in hand and eyes shining, stared longingly at them. Nearby, three men were engaged in the buying and selling of a pig, fattened on acorns, that stood at their feet. It appeared that the priest allowed the people of Lannédern not only to live within the chapel enclosure but also to do business there. Galeran felt comforted to see all this activity around him. He turned again towards the inn.

With its cob walls and its reed thatch, the tavern was a larger building than most of the others in the enclosure. But there was nothing to indicate that it was an inn. Père Gwen and the men of Lannédern went there to eat or drink and to get away from their womenfolk and their bawling children. Only men were allowed in, and when the evening came the innkeeper would ask his wife and daughters to retire once they had prepared the food. Loud voices would then be heard from inside the building, along with roars of anger or astonished exclamations as tales were told of the giant Gwerz or of Edern, the protector of the village.

The tavern comprised three rooms. There was the communal room where the cooking was done and where the customers ate and drank, a bedroom for the innkeeper, his mother, his wife and his two girls, and a second bedroom where straw beds were laid out for pilgrims or travellers. But few guests ever came to this village hidden away in the hills of Arez. Pedlars were the only strangers who ventured there.

An oven had been built next to the inn for the use of the whole village, and it was the innkeeper's responsibility to ensure it remained in good working order.

The only opening to the inn on the side facing the oven was a solid oak door. Once inside, the visitor was immediately struck by the fact that the tavern's one and only window looked directly onto the cemetery. This was a feature which may well have fuelled the frequent conversations held there over the doings of Ankou.

Two long trestle tables, some benches, a large sideboard and a few rough-hewn stools were the only furniture in the main room. The innkeeper had placed a set of flat stones on the earth floor in the centre of the room to serve as the hearth. Black smoke rose up from the fire and passed out through a gaping hole in the roof.

A few old men, their woollen caps pulled down almost over their eyes, sat on stools around the fire and wove thin cord from straw. Near them sat an old woman, probably the innkeeper's mother, abstractedly fulling wool. Wooden bowls had been placed on the tables, for mealtime was approaching. Resin candles gave off a dim light.

The first thing Galeran saw when he walked in was a girl placing two tankards on a table in front of some peasants. If this was the dirty and ugly girl that Drogon had spoken of, then he was clearly being very sarcastic.

The drinkers cut short their conversation when the knight approached them.

'I greet you,' said Galeran. 'I have come to speak with the innkeeper.'

At this the peasants returned to what they had been doing, the old men to their cord, the drinkers to their tankards. The old woman with the wool had not even lifted her head.

'What do you want, sir?' asked the girl, wiping her hands on her tunic.

Galeran had been struck by the beauty of the village women. They were slight, with hair as dark as the brown turf,

74

and eyes grey like mist. Their white smocks set off the melancholy of their gentle faces. But the girl that stood before him now was even prettier than the others he had seen in Lannédern. She barely came up to his chest and her waist was so slim he could have encircled it with his hands. Her white bonnet framed a face so pure it left the knight momentarily speechless. Her lovely grey eyes were red from crying.

'Are you Armelle?' asked Galeran, greeting the girl courteously.

'Yes, sir. That is my name. I shall fetch my father.'

'Stay a moment, I beg you,' said the knight, placing his hand on her arm. 'I would like to ask you some questions about your sister.'

'I can tell you nothing, except that she died a cruel death,' muttered Armelle, pulling herself away from Galeran.

'Forgive me, I did not mean to distress you, mademoiselle. Can you tell me what you know about Broérec's sons?'

The question provoked a little cry, like the sound of an animal caught in a trap.

'You came here with the Lord of Huelgoat! Why then would I talk to you of his sons? Do you think an innkeeper's daughter like me can teach you something you have not already learned by being in their company?'

'What does Drogon have against you?'

Galeran cursed himself for his clumsiness as soon as the question left his lips. The girl's face hardened and she began fiddling with the buttons on her smock.

'He wants to get me with child,' she eventually replied, her grey eyes fixed on the knight's.

At that moment the innkeeper came over to the knight and the girl took the opportunity to slip away.

'Welcome, sir,' said the innkeeper. 'May I offer you a drink?'

'I thank you. Tell me, is your wife feeling better?'

'She is. She has gone to the chapel to pray and to prepare Fanchon's body for burial. You have spoken with Armelle?'

'Yes, and I fear I have offended her. Please tell her I wish her no harm.'

'Armelle is too soft-hearted. But that will pass. What can I do for you, knight?'

'I wanted to ask your daughter about Drogon and about the day her sister disappeared. But I shall return later to speak with her. Good day to you, and may God shield you and yours.'

'Farewell, sir.'

As Galeran left the inn he spotted Armelle making towards the woods. She ran like a hunted deer, and the knight again cursed himself for having upset her. He heard a familiar whinny and turned to see a man-at-arms leading Quolibet to him.

'Sir Broérec says he will wait for you in the château,' said the soldier. 'I am to accompany you.'

'Well then, we should not keep the Lord of Huelgoat waiting,' replied Galeran, who was beginning to find his host's solicitude a little inhibiting.

He climbed into his saddle, and the man-at-arms mounted his own steed, a small warhorse of the type favoured by Bretons.

13

The boy had lost his usual calm and paced up and down the room. His furrowed brow and blazing eyes revealed his anger.

'But why will you not let me go out?' he asked in exasperation.

'You must not expose yourself to attack. These men have blood on their hands. They are impure and they will sully you, Kaourintin.'

'God is my witness that I have no fear of them, Withénoc.'

Kaourintin, unlike the rest of the peasants, was extremely pale of skin. His hair was short and curly, his eyes limpid. He gave a strange impression of clarity of spirit as well as great strength of will. Withénoc avoided his eye.

'My duty is to protect you, even if that means protecting you against yourself,' said the monk.

'Soon there will be thirty of us and the villagers will no longer be able to feed us, not even in exchange for our labour.'

'We shall soon be leaving this place.'

'You can't keep me in a cage for ever, Withénoc!'

'But you are not a prisoner! I seek only to do what is right for you, Kaourintin.'

'I must speak to the children. It's time to leave, the fine days are nearly over.'

'Not now! Do you hear me?'

The monk's tone had changed, had become menacing. The young man sat down on the straw he used as a bed and spoke no more. The more time he spent with the monk, the stranger and the more disturbing he found him.

When Kaourintin had left everything – his home village of Daoulas, his family, his flock – to go preaching on the roads of Brittany he had never thought his crusade would attract so many followers. There were only four or five at the beginning, and now there were dozens. They were children who believed in God, who believed in a celestial Jerusalem, who would no longer put up with the misery of their lives. Boys in search of adventure, girls for whom the mere word Orient was like a dream – they had all fled their homes to go on this crusade, their Crusade. The light they saw in Kaourintin and his beautiful words had inflamed their hearts and they had joined with him, they said, to free the Holy Lands.

Then one day, when Kaourintin was preaching in the marketplace at Carhaix, this man dressed as a monk from Cluny had come to offer his help and his faith. The boy was flattered at the offer from a man of the cloth, and one from Cluny at that, and had gladly accepted Frère Withénoc's assistance.

But their relations had gradually become strained over the four months they had been together. Kaourintin had had to bend to the monk's will and lead his troop of children to this forlorn hamlet in the hills of Arez. Fortunately the villagers had given them a warm welcome. They gave them a barn to sleep in and food in exchange for their labour. The women of the village were especially moved by the ardent faith of these youthful crusaders.

But there was something strange about the whole affair. Kaourintin was certain that Withénoc had known the village priest for a long time, even if the monk never admitted it.

Père Gwen was a gentle man, but the mere presence of Withénoc seemed to paralyse him with fear. The monk for his part was always following the priest and spying on him. So much so that the young shepherd had not managed, in the three months he had been here, to speak privately with Père Gwen. Even in the rare moments when Withénoc was absent, the priest would flee the boy as though he were a leper.

Another troubling thing was the children who disappeared without a trace. It was normal in such a situation that some of the children would become discouraged and desert, but Kaourintin could not understand why Janik of Saint-Herbot's boys should leave him. They had been such fervent believers in God and in the Crusade. Kaourintin had even secretly gone back to Saint-Herbot to see if the two boys had returned. But they had not.

A powerful hand was laid upon his shoulder, and the boy gave a start.

'Forgive me, I have been hard on you,' said Withénoc. 'I promised to help you, but you must give me the means to do so. I do not like Broérec nor his sons. Nor, indeed, this knight, who is too inquisitive for my liking.'

'I do not like Broérec's boy any more than you,' said Kaourintin, thinking of the sweet Armelle who was forced to flee from the brute when he sought to exercise his *droit du seigneur* as though she were a mere serf.

'Come, Kaourintin, let us go back to the children. The men-at-arms have gone.'

The pair left the room. The children ran to them immediately, taking Kaourintin by the hand and leading him to a byre at the far end of the enclosure. It was made entirely of wood and could house up to thirty goats. A platform had been built to store fodder for the winter, and it was here that Kaourintin's little band lodged. Apart from two or three who were ill and who had been taken into the villagers' homes, all the children slept here among the bales of hay. There were twenty-two of them, but more arrived all the time, drawn by some mysterious force.

Kaourintin climbed nimbly up the ladder into the upper part of the byre. There were children everywhere, stretched out on the hay or playing dice on the floor. Some of the younger ones were still yawning, with sleep in their eyes.

The women of the village had that morning brought some pancakes and goat's milk. The cries of the village lookout and the arrival of the Lord of Huelgoat had perturbed everyone. Despite Withénoc's orders not to show themselves, some of the children had gone out to see what was happening before running back to hide in the byre.

When the shepherd boy arrived many of them stood up and went to touch him and kiss his hands.

'Kaourintin, when shall we leave for Jerusalem?' asked a little girl who held onto his sleeve.

'Soon, my dear,' replied Kaourintin, stroking her cheek with his hand. 'Soon, I promise you.'

He sat down on a bale of straw in the middle of the byre, as was his habit. The girl came with some others to sit at his feet. Some of the children hung from the wooden beams supporting the roof to get a better view of their leader. All watched attentively.

'We have been here for months!' declared Goranton, who, like Kaourintin, hailed from Daoulas. 'Why stay any longer?'

'The people here are very good to us,' said a girl, 'but when the winter comes they will no longer need us to work in the fields or mind their animals. They will soon tire of our presence. So let us go. It is in the Holy Lands that we are needed. You yourself have said the voyage will be long and dangerous, so why wait any longer?'

A murmur of agreement spread through the assembly.

'Anna is right. Let us go, Kaourintin! Guide us to Jerusalem.'

'Withénoc says we should stay here,' pleaded the shepherd.

'It is not Withénoc that we are following, it is you!' Goranton retorted heatedly. The children, who both disliked and feared the monk, stamped their feet in approval.

'You are right, Goranton,' said Kaourintin. 'But Withénoc says we must give others the chance to join us here before we leave. And many of you had a perilous journey here and need time to rest.'

'I know all that because you've already said it so many times. But I say that three months is too long and with winter on the way we must go now!'

'We mustn't get stuck here during the dark months, the

villagers won't be able to feed us any more!' proclaimed another boy, who looked about fourteen.

'Those who were sick are getting better now,' said Goranton. 'But we will carry them if we have to, won't we, boys?'

'Yes, yes!' cried the children.

'Do you think we want to turn back now, Kaourintin?'

A litle girl, who had come from Braspartz along with her brother a week ago, burst into tears. Her brother took her in his arms to comfort her, then spoke to Kaourintin in a reproachful tone.

'She's afraid we will have to go back,' he said. 'We ran away to join you, and if we return now the lord will kill us. We do not want to be his serfs. We are free, Kaourintin, we are the children of God. You must guide us!'

Kaourintin, moved by these words, was about to respond when Withénoc appeared on the platform. The monk had clearly heard all that had been said, for when he spoke it was in a voice that sought to be friendly but which revealed his irritation.

'So you really want to leave?'

'Yes,' chorused the children.

'Very well, let us go then.'

'What?' exclaimed Kaourintin. 'But just now you were saying . . .'

'I have changed my mind. I think you and the others are right!'

'You have brought me great happiness, Withénoc.'

Kaourintin then turned to the children.

'The Orient awaits us. The Holy Land! Ultreia! Ultreia!' he cried.

Roars of enthusiasm and much stamping of feet met his words. He stood up, held his hands out to the children and began to recite.

'I see a new sky, a new land. Here God lives among men. He will wipe the tears from their eyes. Death will be no more, nor sorrow nor pain, for the old world will be gone.'

The children knelt around the young shepherd and looked up at him, their eyes wide with wonder.

'He will show me the holy city of Jerusalem, wherein the glory of the Lord is visible. The city shines likes the most precious of diamonds. It needs light neither from the sun nor from the moon, for the splendour of God illuminates it. Nothing that is blemished may enter into it, nor those who have committed abominations.'

PART THREE

Only thou shalt not eat the blood thereof;
thou shalt pour it upon the ground as water.

Deuteronomy 15.23

14

Broérec flung open Galeran's bedroom door before dawn the next morning and threw a tunic, breeches and a cloak of indeterminate colour onto his bed.

'You can wear this for the hunt,' he grunted. 'They belonged to our old tracker. I think they've never been washed, so you'll smell just as nice as the beasts we hunt. Even with my poor sense of smell I can tell you that they stink. He used to rub deer dung all over them.'

'Used to?'

'He was gored by a stag at the last hunt.'

'You're giving me these clothes so I can pass unnoticed?'

'It was Drogon's idea.'

'Well, I think I would rather wear my own clothes. I can rub them with soil and grass, as we do in Léon before we go hunting. Let Drogon do whatever he is accustomed to, and I shall so likewise.'

'You are right, you should do as you wish.'

'Have you seen Jestin since yesterday?'

'No,' replied the giant, his face suddenly sombre. 'He did not sleep here last night. I'm worried, for he has been gone since yesterday morning.'

'Concern for another is not sentiment I hear you express very often,' remarked Galeran. 'Come Broérec, surely this is not the first time your boy has spent the night away from home?'

'It is not. But as you will have seen, Jestin is not at all like his brother. And he has always come to bid me farewell before he goes off. I find his absence troubling. What if he has come to the same end as these children?'

'Be reasonable! He has only been gone since yesterday.'

'Perhaps,' grumbled Broérec. 'But last night I couldn't stop thinking about what you said to me yesterday. God's wounds! All these deaths, all these children disappearing. I swear to you, I did not know the extent of this.'

'Listen, Broérec. The bodies were of people much younger than Jestin. And they were peasant children, not the sons and daughters of a lord. But we shall speak of that later. Your boy is a handsome chap. Has he not perhaps gone to see some pretty girl in a neighbouring village?'

The giant shook his head.

'He's not one for chasing after girls. He lives like a monk.'

Galeran was struck by the fact that Jestin seemed to be the only person in the world for whom Broérec had any concern. Perhaps he was the only one that he loved.

'What about Drogon?' he asked. 'He was not there either when we got back from Lannédern. Were they together?'

'Those two? Huh! They fight like cats and dogs. They hate each other. I knew Drogom would be gone by the time we got back. He usually disappears for a while before we go hunting.'

'Why is that?'

'He and Thustan always like to prepare themselves well for the hunt.'

'What do you mean?' asked Galeran, as he placed his leather cloak over his tunic.

'You'll see. Are you ready?'

'Yes.'

'You shall have one of my best bows and some fine arrows. You're not a bad archer, if my memory is correct.'

'You remember that old boar that gave us so much trouble in Vitré?'

'He was a tough old brute. Your arrow found him but he kept on charging at us even though he was dead!' said Broérec, slapping Galeran on the back.

They had reached the lower courtyard, and the knight now understood what his host had meant when he spoke of

Drogon's preparations. The youth stood there, unrecognisable, wearing only a leather belt around his waist from which hung a long cutlass. He was covered from head to foot in dark clay – even his beard and his blond hair were smeared with earth. He looked like a savage as he strode, his muscles tensing, up and down the yard.

'Greetings, Drogon,' said Galeran.

Drogon, whose body gave off a fetid odour, did not reply. He looked at the knight but gave no sign of recognition. His pupils were dilated as though he were under the influence of some drug.

Broérec led Galeran to the gate, where he showed him a line of bows leaning against a wall.

'It's this one,' he said, handing the knight a short bow and a quiver of arrows with blue fledging.

Galeran took the bow and examined it. It was indeed a finely crafted weapon. He bent it to check its resistance and looked in the quiver to make sure there was some spare string. Then he slipped it over his shoulder and took the arrows from the quiver to examine their heads.

'How do you like it?' asked Broérec.

'I am impressed. It has a fine curve and I would guess it shoots far. I thank you.'

'Here,' said Broérec, handing him a leather glove. 'It's Jestin's. It should fit you.'

Galeran slipped the glove on his right hand, checked that he had his dagger with him, and declared himself ready.

Thustan arrived with the mastiffs straining at their leashes. He too was almost naked and covered in clay. He marched up to Broérec and whispered something in his ear. He wore a only an axe, hanging from the black cloth belt that circled his waist, and a hunting horn slung around his shoulder. Like Drogon, he had tied his hair up so that it would not trouble him during the hunt.

Galeran had heard tell of hunters who chased their prey

naked, but he had thought it was something that was done only on the other side of the Rhine. Perhaps Broérec's beautiful Valkyrie had told them of the Germanic tradition.

'I wouldn't like to meet this crowd on a dark night,' thought the knight, remembering his father's warnings. 'One would think they had gone back to their pagan roots.'

'Thustan knows where the stag is,' said Broérec. 'Two leagues from here. He says it is one that has escaped us many times. There will be just the four of us for this hunt. Thustan will do the tracking. And it will probably be Drogon who does the killing, for that is what he likes most.'

'Who knows?' replied Galeran.

15

The drawbridge was lowered and the four men filed out of the château. Thustan led the way with the dogs, his bare feet scarcely making a sound on the damp ground. The forest was still dark but the grey light of dawn was beginning to seep through the foliage. The hunters advanced quickly. The only noise to be heard was the plaintive cry of birds announcing the arrival of the day. Galeran noted that they were taking the path that led to the Roman road to Carhaix, but Thustan soon veered off to the right.

'Listen!' said Thustan, who had suddenly stopped in his tracks. 'It is him.'

The birds had fallen silent and from a distance came the wild cry of a stag in rut. It was difficult to know just how far away the beast was, for its resonant call could travel several leagues.

Galeran felt his heart beating faster. The stag's call was like a war cry in its savage intensity, and no man could hear it without being troubled.

The two mastiffs stood with their noses to the wind. They trembled with impatience, waiting for a sign from their master, who had taken their chains from Thustan.

The hunting party moved on and soon found itself on a broader path that wound its way through rocks. The vegetation here was much less dense.

Suddenly, Thustan shot off ahead of the others. Galeran was astounded that a man so short and stocky could run so fast. The dogs strained on their chains but Drogon held them tight.

The rest of the party soon caught up with Thustan, who had stopped at the edge of a clearing. In the middle of the clearing was a pond whose banks showed traces of animals that had visited in the night. Drogon let the dogs off their chains and they ran to sniff around the pond before returning at their master's whistle. Drogon then tied their leashes to a solid tree trunk and with a brief command quieted them. They lay down with their heads on their paws, their eyes shining ferociously.

'Why did he bring them if he's going to leave them here?' Galeran asked of Broérec.

'Drogon has sworn that no beast will ever escape him. He never takes the dogs with him when he is hunting this stag. But if it were to kill him, then he has told us to let the dogs keep his promise for him.'

'I see,' murmured Galeran.

They set off, leaving the dogs in the clearing. The stag could not be far away now. They had been on the move for several hours, and sweat ran down Galeran's face and chest. But the thrill of the chase prevented him from feeling the fatigue that was slowly seeping through his muscles.

Thustan gave a sign and the men stopped. A wind had come up, which could be an advantage for the hunters or could reveal their presence to the stag if it blew in the animal's direction. Drogon, signalling to the others to lie down, knelt next to Thustan. The pair were obviously in charge of the hunt, a fact which surprised Galeran, who had never before seen Broérec renouncing his leadership.

Before them was a rocky hill covered in dense vegetation.

'The herd is on the hill,' said Broérec, lying down to place his ear against the ground. 'The wind is in our favour, but we should wait a while to see if it does not turn.'

From above them came a raucous bell. The stag had perhaps scented another male approaching. Then came the sound of branches crashing, a heavy trampling, and shriller cries from younger deer in the large herd. Another powerful bell sounded.

'Do you hear how deep it is?' asked Galeran.

'Yes, he must be old. Perhaps it is the one that killed my tracker. That was an enormous brute.'

Thustan, followed closely by Drogon, began crawling towards the hill. They slid like snakes over the ground. Broérec and Galeran caught up with them in a small clearing, the higher part of which was sealed off with brambles. It was an ideal place to shoot the stag, for the beast would be slowed here by the undergrowth.

The four men stood up silently. Thustan told the others to withdraw a little. He alone remained in the middle of the clearing. He slowly raised his horn to his lips. Drogon nocked an arrow in his bow, then signalled to his father and Galeran to stand next to him.

Galeran took two arrows and put them under his left foot so that he might fire more quickly without letting the target out of his sight. All three now tensed their bows in readiness, aiming towards the brambles at the top of the clearing.

Thustan began stamping his foot and striking a tree trunk with the flat of his axe to imitate the sounds of a male in rut. Then he gave another call on his horn, a call that was harsher than the last, and almost indistinguishable from the sound of a mating stag. He knew his prey would not be attracted by a cry that was too shrill, for this was the sign of an adversary that was young and weak. But a deep call meant an older male, one he could not ignore.

They did not have to wait long for a reaction to the horn. A long and guttural bell echoed through the trees. Silence followed, as though the forest itself held its breath. Then came a sound like an avalanche of stones rolling down towards them. The furious beast smashed all before it as it rushed to face its enemy.

The acrid smell of the rutting beast swept over them as the stag burst into the clearing and charged at Thustan, who rolled to one side while the three archers let fly their metal shafts. Its back covered in sweat, its eyes bulging, its teeth ready to tear into its enemy, the beast continued its charge, the arrows protruding from its flank.

Neither Galeran nor Broérec had time to fire again. They watched, unable to intervene, as Drogon threw his bow to the ground and ran screaming at the stag. The animal suddenly seemed disconcerted at the presence of humans and hesitated a moment before continuing its attack. Galeran dropped his bow and reached for his cutlass.

When the antlers were within inches of him, Drogon stepped to one side, rammed his knife into the beast's side and hung from it with all his weight. The momentum of the stag's charge carried them on through the clearing for some distance before the beast fell to the ground with a last cry. Dark blood spurted from its flank and neck.

Drogon pulled his knife out of the wound and began slashing at the stag's neck. Maddened by the sight of blood, he placed his lips over one of the gashes he had made and avidly began to drink the blood. A nauseating smell came from the animal.

Broérec stood, a troubled light in his eye, and watched his son kneeling by the stag. Drogon eventually stood up, his mouth red and the bloody dagger still in his hand. His father walked slowly towards the kill. He plunged his index finger into the wound, turned to his son and with the blood drew a cross on his forehead.

Thustan had not moved during the clash. Now he cut three branches of oak to pay homage both to the beast and to the man who had killed it. He dipped the branches in blood and placed the first along the stag's spine and the second as a last meal between its teeth; the third he gave to Drogon.

Galeran had heard tell of this ancient custom practised by Germanic hunters during the reign of Conrad III. He picked up his arrows and put them back in the quiver before going to inspect the dead stag. At that moment Drogon plunged his knife into the animals' belly and its entrails poured out onto the ground. Apparently oblivious to the stench, he cleaned out the stomach and cut off the testicles to offer them to his father, stepping aside to let Thustan carve up the beast. More blood gushed out to stain the grass and spread its bitter smell through the air. Galeran and Drogon helped the man at his work. When the task was done the knight wiped himself down, looking over at Broérec as he did so.

The giant sat, deep in thought, on a fallen tree trunk. Galeran suddenly realised how much he had changed over the ten years he had spent at Vitré. He still displayed the same arrogance and bravado, but it was clear that inside him something had snapped. Never before would he have taken second place in the hunt or in the carving up of the kill.

It suddenly came to Galeran that Broérec saw Drogon as his most dangerous rival. The man might be a brute, but he was a cunning one. When he had sent for Galeran it may well have been so that the knight could protect him from his own son. If Galeran had not been present at the hunt today, might it not have ended tragically? And without witnesses?

He looked again at Broérec. The kill had brought him no joy. The superb stag had reigned for a long time over its herd, beating off younger rivals with its superior strength. But it had taken moments to put an end to its domination, and now the beast was no more than a bloody heap of bones over which Drogon's dogs would soon be fighting.

'It is curious,' he mumbled, glancing at Galeran. 'Hunting is no longer a pleasure for me.'

Thustan brought the mastiffs and let them loose on the carcass and the entrails. Then he took the cloth belt that he wore around his waist and with it wrapped offal from the stag. He distributed the meat among the four of them to carry back to the château. Drogon took the antlers and placed them on his broad shoulders. He resembled Cernunnos, the god of Celts.

They headed for home, Broérec still sombre and silent, Drogon staggering with fatigue. Thustan stayed behind with the dogs as they finished off the carcass.

16

The day was well advanced by the time they got back to the château. Broérec immediately enquired whether Jestin had returned, and, on learning that he had not, withdrew without a word to his bed with a large jug of his baneful drink. Drogon also took to his bed to sleep off the intoxication of the hunt and the dark blood he had drunk. Thustan and a manservant carried the meat to the larder.

Galeran, for his part, went to visit Quolibet to check that he had been given food and water. He had, so the knight contented himself with changing his bedding. Then he washed at the cistern and went into the keep to take off his muddy and bloodstained clothes.

When he got to his room he immediately saw that someone had been looking through his possessions. His seal and his money were still in his pouch, but the parchment Broérec had sent to summon him was gone.

'Yet there was little of import written there,' he mused.

He could not see how anyone could have been interested in it. Then it occurred to him that the theft might be a warning.

'We shall see,' he told himself. 'In the meantime, I must eat. I shall track down old Cléophas and see if he can make me something edible.'

He climbed down the ladder to the kitchen, where he saw a tranquil figure sitting in semi-darkness near the hearth. It was Cléophas, who turned and looked at him in slight irritation. In one hand he held a large sausage rolled up in a pancake and in the other a knife.

'Well, Master Cléophas, I see you are having a feast!' said Galeran gaily.

The man mischievously screwed up his little grey eyes and with his knife pointed up at the ceiling.

'They're all asleep. That's how it is every time they go hunting – drunk as lords. I'll have peace now until tomorrow morning. But you, sir, you don't drink any of that liquor that smells of the piss of animals.'

He made as if to get up.

'I'll serve you upstairs,' he said.

'Not at all, Cléophas,' said Galeran, lowering himself onto the bench beside the old man. 'I shall share your meal, which looks excellent and, I might add, much better than the fare your master likes.'

Cléophas got up and went over to a large wooden salting tub. He removed the lid and took out half a smoked ham and some pancakes and handed the lot to Galeran.

'You know,' he said, 'I've had it up to here with game. It ruins the stomach. It's poison, all that dark blood. Can kill you, even. Here, sir, help yourself. My wife sent me this from the farm.'

Galeran took from his pouch a flask of eau-de-vie and handed it to Cléophas, who threw back his head and drank the fiery liquid as though it were water. He nodded, then wiped his mouth with his sleeve.

'That's warmed me up!' he said, and gave a satisfied belch.

'It's from Léon, my home,' said Galeran as he cut himself some thick slices of ham, placed them on a pancake and wolfed them down.

Cléophas ate slowly. He cut his food into small pieces which he swallowed without chewing, for he had no teeth left.

'Tomorrow I shall go to the hamlet,' said Galeran. 'Can I give your wife a message from you?'

'Alas, my Génovéfa is there and I am here . . . Broérec won't have any women in the château.'

'I know. But is there anything you want me to tell her?'

'My wife is not in the village, sir. She's with my son at the farm, which is near the village.'

The old man took the knight's arm and looked thought-fully into his eyes.

'I know you have come because of the children, and I for my part worry about Jestin ... But it is best not to say anything here, the walls have ears.'

He paused for a moment, nodding his head as though he felt he had made himself clear.

'I shall send my helper, Titik, to tell my wife you are coming. She knows a few things and might be able to help you. A very agreeable woman she is too,' he added with a sigh.

'I thank you, Cléophas,' said Galeran as he stood up. 'But you should not torment yourself. Broérec is how he is, he needs to make war on everybody.'

'I know. And he's not as bad as his demon of a father. He loves his sons, which is something. The old man was Satan in person. He died alone in the forest, like a dog. We found him there, and believe me, his villainous face was as dark as if he was already in Hell.'

Cléophas drank another mouthful.

'Broérec suffered a lot at the hands of his father,' he added. 'And when he lost his lady ... I just hope no harm ever comes to Jestin.'

Rancour and hatred were unknown to the man, thought Galeran as he looked at Cléophas. Broérec had degraded and humiliated him, separated him from his wife, and yet he still had sympathy for his master.

'Good old Cléophas!' he said, slapping him on the back. 'For once, your food was excellent. Here, keep my flask.'

The knight climbed up the ladder to his room, stretched out on his bed and within seconds was in a deep sleep.

17

Early the next morning, when the château was still silent, Galeran went to the stables to see to Quolibet. On his way he stopped off in the cellar to take some ham and a pancake. Cléophas did not object, for the good reason that he lay fast asleep on the bench where the knight had left him the night before. Beside him sat the flask of eau-de-vie.

The only person Galeran saw in the courtyard was Thustan, who was crouching down to sharpen his axe. He replied to the knight's greeting with a hostile grunt.

'Not very talkative this morning, Thustan? Thinking of your old friend in the forest?' jibed Galeran as he climbed up into his saddle.

Thustan spat on his blade.

The drawbridge was raised and Galeran rode out. He found the path that led to Loaurn without difficulty, and trotted off towards the hamlet of Huelgoat.

The lookouts had apparently not felt it necessary to signal Galeran's arrival. Plumes of smoke rose from the rooftops and all seemed peaceful in the hamlet. A boy tended his flock near the path. Old women were spreading out washing on the hedges and the grass between the cottages. As Galeran approached two men armed with forks appeared from behind one of the shacks and stood in front of him.

'Where are you for, sir?'

'Good day to you. Where I come from we first exchange greetings. I am a knight from Léon and I come here in peace.'

'We don't like people prowling around, and knights we like even less,' said one of the men, a sturdy, ruddy-faced young chap.

'Old Cléophas led me to believe I would receive a somewhat warmer welcome.'

'Cléophas? He hardly comes at all now to see his wife and son. But never mind that; it was he who sent you?'

'Can you show me where Génovéfa's farm is?'

The two men hesitated. Galeran moved Quolibet forward a little until his head was pushing against the crossed forks.

'Come, I have wasted enough time. Where does the woman live?'

'Go behind the cairns, then it's straight through the wood,' replied the older man, lowering his fork.

'I thank you,' said Galeran, taking his leave of them.

He could feel the hostile eyes of the villagers on his back as he rode through the hamlet, but no one else tried to stop him.

18

The farm was about a league from the hamlet, at the end of an overgrown path. Old trees blown down by winter winds blocked the track at several points; others suffocated by ivy hung menacingly over the fern and nettles that choked the path.

Quolibet jumped over a little mound of earth and Galeran found himself in a well-tended clearing, in the middle of which stood the farm. He was astonished by the size of the building. It looked like an old barn, fortified with granite at the bottom and at the top of its walls with little stones firmly cemented in place. It was clear that the Romans had been here. A dilapidated wall encircled a courtyard in which stood stables with thatched roofs. The ruins of a square tower gave the place an air of sadness and solitude.

Galeran dismounted. The carriage gate was half open, and next to it stood a watching figure. It was a young boy, who walked up to him to greet him eagerly.

'May I take your horse, sir? My mother is waiting for you inside.'

'You are Cléophas's son?'

'I am. My name is Yann.'

He took Quolibet's reins and stroked the horse's neck.

'You have a fine horse, sir. Is he a warhorse?'

The boy looked about fifteen years old. His eyes shone like pearls.

'He is indeed a warhorse,' said Galeran. 'But he's good for peace too!'

The main room of the farmhouse was gloomy, lit only by the open door and a narrow window overlooking the yard. But it was paved and well furnished. There were two chests upon which lay some manuscripts and a musical instrument, a psaltery. On the polished table stood a jug and pewter goblets, alongside a plate of nut pancakes and a stoneware dish filled with blackberries.

The hostess stood by the table, dressed in a bright blue tunic taken in at the waist. Her bonnet was immaculately white. Her face was ageless, her skin smooth as a pebble. She seemed amused by Galeran's surprise. But he noticed that her slender hands were trembling, and indeed he too felt nervous. At last he had before him a witness, but he was not yet sure how he should bring her to tell him what she knew without alarming her.

He need not have worried. The woman poured him a glass of mead, invited him to sit down and took a seat across the table from him.

'I made it with the honey from my own bees,' she informed him.

'I believe you make honey differently in these parts?'

'Yes, here we carve out the inside of a tree trunk so that the bees make their hive there.'

Galeran sniffed the drink, brought it to his lips and drank deep. He admitted that he had never drunk better.

The woman got up and closed the door. She leaned out of the window and looked both ways before returning to the table with a sigh of satisfaction.

'You are wondering why I live here, sir?'

'By my faith, Dame Génovéfa, your home does seem isolated for a region as dangerous as this one.'

'It has not always been thus. There used to be a small garrison and a fine earth rampart around the house. Today I have only three farmhands and an old womanservant, but I know of no one that is my enemy.'

'But what about Cléophas?'

She lowered her eyes and fiddled with the gold chain that hung around her neck.

'That old husband of mine?' she said with a vague smile.

'Very well, I see that I shall have to tell you all. First, you should know that my mother was a distant blood-relation of Lord Broérec. She married a rich merchant who came from Bures, near Dives. That too is a marshland, but full of life and not at all wild like the Yeûn. When I was ten my parents and their servants were killed by a band of robbers in the forest of Perche. I was sent to an aunt of my father's. Her name was Emmeline and she lived in Caen near the Abbaye aux Dames. There I learned to read, to count, to make music. And I learned Latin. When Dame Emmeline died she left me all her belongings. I suddenly became rather wealthy for a fifteen-year-old.

'It was then that Broérec made his entrance. He claimed to be my only living relative, and said he would take me into his care. He was very young and handsome at the time. He had just remarried, and he hoped I would keep Dame Mechtilde company and help her run her house.'

'Forgive me, but are you saying that Broérec had been married before?'

'Yes. His first wife died giving birth to that swine Drogon.'

'So that's it,' murmured the knight.

'Yes, that's it,' she echoed.

'But please, go on. This is of the utmost importance.'

'Knowing what the château is like today it is hard to imagine how different it was when I was there with Dame Mechtilde. We made the finest meals, we danced, we invited lords and ladies from the whole region. The forest around the château was well looked after and you could stroll there without any danger. The land was fruitful, the serfs lived comfortably and were treated well. Cléophas was young and was Broérec's most trusted man. He loved me. And when we married I soon learned that he was a good husband, for he always gave me comfort and support. I had a good dowry and Broérec gave us this farm and the land around as a wedding present.'

Génovéfa's voice now became lifeless, and the colour drained from her face.

'But life is strange, sir,' she went on. 'I never imagined I would see all that happiness, all that love ruined in so short a time.'

She seized her cup of mead and drank it down in one go.

'Do you know what jealousy is, knight?'

'I'm sure . . .'

'I mean real jealousy. It is an intolerable sorrow that you catch like leprosy, that eats away at you.'

She shook her head. Her eyes were the same amber as her son's.

'Broérec caught the malady when he married Mechtilde. She was, as you might expect, not very grateful for being abducted from her family. At first it was hard to see it in him for war kept him away much of the time. But his new wife kept him at an even greater distance and this drove him mad. Have you ever seen someone jealous of the seat his lady sits on? Someone who would kill the horse she liked most? Who would cut the throat of the dog she caressed? That is how he was. He was a man who had forced himself on many a woman, and he was torn by the thought of what his woman did in his absence. The poor devil was punished with his own sin!'

Dame Génovéfa fell silent, and Galeran sensed that her tale was over.

'Madame, I thank you for trusting me,' he said. 'But there is something else I came for. Have you see young Jestin recently? His father is very worried about him.'

'Why should I tell you?' she asked coldly.

'Because I know you look after him and that you even helped bring him into this world.'

'That is true. I also fed him with milk from my breast and taught him to read and write. He is a clever boy, not like his illiterate brute of a brother.'

'Yes,' said Galeran. 'She is very intelligent.'

'What do you mean!' exclaimed Dame Génovéfa.

'Madame, one would need to be blind not to recognise who Jestin really is.'

'What do you want from me, knight?'

'The truth. And your help in saving Jestin's life and the lives of many others besides.'

She shrugged her shoulders.

'Very well then. Listen to me, and listen well, for I shall not speak of this again. You know that Broérec has driven all women from his château, and that he has fallen under the influence of that monster Thustan. Well, he always respected me because I stood up to him. But I soon had enough and left the château to come here. His revenge was to take almost all responsibility away from Cléophas and make him little more than a cook.'

'All that I can well believe. But what about Broérec's unfortunate wife?'

'The poor woman could breathe only when he was away. But she knew that he would soon be the death of her, for he had taken to drink and was prone to the most terrible rages. He was away waging war somewhere when she was due to give birth for the first time, so she came to me here at the farm. I delivered the baby, with Cléophas's help. But when we saw the sex of the child we did not know which way to turn.

'But I should have said that a few days beforehand, Siegfried, one of her cousins, had also arrived at the farm. I had seen him the last time he was in our land, a year before. He was from the province of Harz, where Mechtilde herself came from, and was accompanied by thirty mounted men armed to the teeth. Well, at least they said he was her cousin. But what I am sure of is that he was tall and handsome like the Archangel and that he was the most gentle of men when he was with her. And what I also know is that, five days after the birth, Mechtilde and Siegfried were gone and the only one left was little Ninian. I was still nursing my own boy, who was six months old at the time, so I fed her too. And then we decided that Ninian would become Jestin.'

'How did Broérec react to his wife's disappearance?'

'It knocked him senseless. But at the same time I think he was relieved, like a sick man who suddenly finds himself cured of his illness.'

'Did you tell him about the strange cousin?'

'No, I certainly did not. I simply said she had disappeared and that we couldn't find her anywhere, that perhaps she was in Youdik. But he just shook his head and replied like the pagan he is: "Even if she's in Hell I shall find her!" I shall never forget the way he looked at me, and I prayed that he would never discover her. Even today he still looks for her, going out at night with that werewolf Thustan. When they hear the pair of them riding through the darkness, the peasants think it's the Devil's own hunting party.'

'So,' thought Galeran, 'ten years ago when he was singing her praises the good lady had already been gone for quite a while. And now he pretends that she is dead . . .'

'We kept the girl with us for a long time. It never even occurred to Broérec that it might not be a boy. He took to the child. In fact, he was captivated, and would visit as often as he could. And Ninian played the role remarkably well. She was always livelier and more robust than my son. And then one day Broérec came and took her to the château.'

Galeran stood up and went to sit next to her.

'You love this child,' he said. 'Do you know that she is in great danger?'

The woman shuddered.

'No,' she murmured. 'She will be safe as long as I say nothing.'

'But you are also in danger, you know too much. Why will you not leave this place? You have the means to go and live in a town with your son and your husband, who is a free man. Or you could tell me the rest of the story!'

Dame Génovéfa shook her head sombrely and Galeran knew she would say no more.

19

The villagers of Saint-Herbot had been warned of the knight's arrival by the lookouts, and now stood blocking his path. Galeran reined in his mount and found himself in the middle of a circle of hostile men and women bearing forks and cudgels.

The tragic deaths of little Fanchon and of the other child had incensed them. The villagers had been living in fear for months and this was the last straw. They had put up with the bullying and insults of Broérec and his henchmen for too long. Now they were no longer afraid, and they were driven by a fierce hatred of the man they saw as their worst enemy.

Galeran sensed this and wondered if their aggression would turn against him.

'Peace be with you,' he said, moving Quolibet forward a little. 'I am Galeran de Lesneven, a knight from Léon, and I have come to help you.'

'Prove it,' shouted an old man, shaking his fist at him. 'You were with Lord Broérec and his damned son yesterday, we saw you.'

A murmur of approval spread through the crowd.

'If you doubt me, then ask Père Gwen of Lannédern. He will vouch for me.'

The priest's name seemed to calm the mob.

'I have come to find out who has committed these crimes. I want to know who killed Fanchon and all the other innocent children, and I need your help.'

'You are a friend of Drogon,' said a man, exhibiting the stump of an arm that had been mauled by Drogon's dogs. 'This is how he collects his taxes!'

'I am no one's friend. My king is Christ and His justice, and I am His knight. I have come to find the man who is doing the killing and to punish him. If that man is Broérec's son or even Broérec himself, then he will be punished.'

The peasants were impressed with these words and by the knight's severe mien. They moved aside to let through an old man in a brown tunic. He told them to disperse, and they moved off in silence.

'I greet you, knight. Please forgive the less than warm welcome you have received, and come to my house. I am Gweltaz Ar Fur, and the people here consider me their chief.'

The man had a dignified air. His face was wrinkled and he wore a long white beard in the Carolingian style. His pale grey eyes looked without expression at the knight. He led Galeran into the little chapel that served as his home and shut the door behind them.

'Let us be frank. You are looking for the murderer, and we too want to find him. How can we help you?'

'I would like you to tell me your version of what has been going on.'

'Please sit down,' said the old man, pointing to a bench where he himself now also sat.

He began his tale. His first few sentences told Galeran nothing he did not already know. But then he said that since Cléophas had lost his job as intendant, Drogon had taken it upon himself to collect Broérec's dues. He would demand the same tax twice, would set his dogs on anyone who dared stand up to him, and would even rape the women of the village. Only Lannédern, which was protected by the fact that it was on consecrated ground and by the presence of Père Gwen, could still resist the young lord's manoeuvres. Drogon had not been so blatant in his misdeeds since his father had returned, but he had managed to persuade Broérec to make his role as indentant official.

Gweltaz knew the peasants needed to be united to face these assaults, and had set up a network of lookouts who watched the tracks and the château night and day. Thus it was that when Galeran visited Huelgoat and Saint-Herbot with Broérec and his men, they found the villages deserted, with not even a goat left to plunder.

But Gweltaz also knew that things could not go on like this. It would not be long before the peasants decided to deal with Broérec and his son once and for all.

'You have not spoken of Broérec's second son, Jestin,' said Galeran. 'What do you make of him?'

'Ah, Jestin, he's a stealthy one. He just appears and you never see him coming. He was raised by Dame Génovéfa and, like her, he has much sympathy for us. And we have great respect for him. Last winter he came here with a cart loaded with turf so that we should not freeze to death. Neither his father nor Drogon knew of it. Jestin is a good man.'

'Have you seen him recently?'

'No. Why?'

'He hasn't been back to the château since yesterday morning. Promise me, Gweltaz, that if you or your lookouts spot him you will tell me.'

'I swear it.'

'Who were the children who disappeared from your village?'

'Janik's two sons, two lads aged twelve and fourteen, and a boy from Huelgoat.'

'Did anything strange happen at the time when they disappeared?'

'Not that I recall,' replied Gweltaz, frowning.

'Think about it. And if you do remember anything, let me know through Titik, the boy who works with Cléophas. He goes often to Génovéfa's farm.'

'You have met Génovéfa?'

'Yes, today. Cléophas is a lucky chap.'

'True. He was a fine-looking man in his day.'

'I don't think Génovéfa is safe at the farm. She is too isolated there.'

'True again. Many times have I invited her to come here with her boy, but she always says no. She is very stubborn.'

'If you agree, I think that we should insist upon it. I shall ask her myself to come here in the interests of her son, for my presence makes the danger she faces all the more serious.'

'She will be well received, that I promise you. But why should your being here make any difference?'

'I think the murderers know the hunt has begun and that they themselves could soon become the prey. And that, naturally, does not greatly please them.'

'We shall do whatever we can to help you, knight.'

'I know you will, Gweltaz Ar Fur,' said Galeran as he got to his feet.

The old man paused for a moment and his face grew suddenly anxious.

'There is something which I have just thought of . . .'

'Yes?'

'Well, it's that shepherd Kaourintin, who is living in Lannédern. He has a band of children with him, and I wonder where they all come from.'

'I have been wondering about him too. What do you think of the boy?'

'He seems sincere. But I cannot say the same about that man who follows him around. He's as dark as the boy is light.'

'Père Gwen told me Kaourintin has been visited by God.'

'More than that, sir! The boy is calling for a new Crusade. He wants to take the children to the Holy Land. He has no care for the danger nor for the sorrow of the parents.'

'To the Holy Land?'

'Yes. I am astounded that people let their children go. Unless . . .'

'Unless they ran away to join him and they are from places far from here,' sighed the knight. 'I must get to Lannédern without delay. I have a bad feeling about this. Farewell, my friend.'

'God shield you, knight.'

20

When Galeran arrived in Lannédern he knew that something had changed.

There seemed to be fewer people around than the last time he was here. He saw Père Gwen walking towards him.

'They have left, have they not?' he asked.

'Yes, my son,' replied the priest, greeting him.

'Forgive me, Father. I am forgetting how to be civil. I have the feeling that those children are the key to your torments.'

'What do you mean, knight?'

Galeran jumped down from his horse, tied the reins to a tree and took the priest by the arm.

'Tell me about Withénoc.'

The old man turned pale but did not speak.

'He has left too, hasn't he?' insisted the knight.

'The man is a demon! And I am guilty of great cowardice.'

'You knew him before?'

The priest hesitated. His hands began to shake uncontrollably.

'The life of these children is at stake, Father,' said Galeran. 'You no longer have the right to remain silent!'

'I do not know much,' Gwen pleaded. 'It was ten years ago, at Landévennec.'

'The Benedictine abbey? What is the connection with Frère Withénoc?'

'Withénoc wore the Benedictine habit at that time. When I met him for the first time he was a prisoner in the abbey.'

'A prisoner?'

'Our parish was linked to Landévennec, and the brother abbot had invited me there. In the scriptorium there was a Bible that was very old and of great value. But the holy book had disappeared. And, what was worse, a monk who was working as a copyist was found dead in the scriptorium. The abbot was sure Withénoc was the guilty party but had no proof against him. So he had him locked up and was going to hand him over to the secular authorities.'

'But?'

'Withénoc must have had accomplices inside the abbey, for one fine morning they found the door of his cell wide open and the bird flown.'

Gwen paused again to draw breath.

'When Withénoc arrived here with Kaourintin I did not recognise him at first. He takes such care to hide his face.'

'But he recognised you?'

'Yes. And I even think that it was not by chance that he picked this village. But then again, in this affair I am sure of nothing. At Landévennec he may well have been falsely accused. I have no right to judge him. But, God forgive me, the man frightens me.'

'What happened after he came here?'

'When he was certain that I knew his identity he threatened to kill me if I gave him away. And he said he would kill Kaourintin too. So I kept away from him, and from Kaourintin, for that is what Withénoc ordered me to do.'

'What was the boy's role in all this?'

'Kaourintin is pure of soul. He is an innocent.'

'But what can a man like Withénoc want from the boy?'

'Heavens knows, knight. Ask young Armelle. She was close to Kaourintin. Perhaps she knows more than I do.'

'Thank you, Father. May God protect you.'

'It is you who need protection. I shall pray for you, and for myself a little too.'

With these words the priest began walking slowly towards his chapel.

Armelle sat on a stone bench in front of her parents' inn. She did not hear Galeran approach, and he stopped to observe her for a moment.

'Good day to you, mademoiselle.'

The girl gave a start, jumped to her feet and smoothed down her petticoats.

'Good day, sir. I hadn't seen you there.'

'No,' smiled Galeran, 'you were somewhere far away.'

She looked down at the ground and did not reply.

'Do not blush, Armelle. And do not run away like the last time. I need your help.'

'How can I aid you, knight?' she said, her pretty eyes suddenly on his face.

'I must find Kaourintin and the children. I am very concerned about them.'

Armelle paled and put her hand to her breast.

'Has something happened to him?'

'Not that I know of. But I need to speak with him.'

'They left this morning.'

'I know. Père Gwen told me. But which direction did they go in?'

She hesitated a moment, then decided to trust Galeran, and began talking rapidly.

'I met Kaourintin last night. He told me they were leaving at dawn. I wanted to go with them but he refused. He knows my parents need me more than ever now that Fanchon is gone. He told me he had quarrelled with Withénoc. He doesn't trust him any more but he doesn't know how to get rid of him. He's afraid of him.'

'Which road did they take?'

'They didn't take any road. I got up early to bid them farewell but they were already gone. The lookouts said they went through the forest towards Roc'h Begheor. I ran and tried to catch up with them. But the funny thing was that they caught up with me!'

'What do you mean, Armelle?'

'I lost their trail and was about to turn back when I heard the noise of breaking branches in front of me. I hid in the bushes and then I saw them coming towards me.'

'They had turned back?'

'They were going in the direction of Ar Menez Reûn. They must have done a big loop.'

'Did you tell Kaourintin this?'

'I didn't dare speak to him. He was walking next to the monk, so I stayed in my hiding place.'

'Do you think he knew what was going on?'

'Perhaps. Kaourintin is not from here but he has a very good sense of direction. It's that horrible monk who is up to no good.'

'So what did you do?'

'I came back home. My mother has been so poorly since Fanchon's death.'

'I must go now, Armelle. But one last question. Have you seen Jestin lately?'

'No, sir, I have not.'

'He has not returned to the château and no one seems to know where he is. Please tell everyone here that I am looking for him. Gweltaz Ar Fur will tell you how to reach me.'

'You have seen Gweltaz?'

'Yes. And I am counting on him as an ally, just as I am on you, Armelle.'

'Yes, sir. Bring back Kaourintin and the children, I beg you!' she said, nervously rubbing her hands together.

'You must be calm, mademoiselle. I shall find them. But now I must return to the château. Take care, my sweet.'

With a mischievous smile he gently took her chin in his hand.

'Does Kaourintin know that you love him?'

'Oh, sir!' exclaimed Armelle.

Then she went on in a voice that was little more than a whisper.

'No, he does not. He thinks only of God.'

As Galeran rode off he turned to cast one last look at the village and saw that Armelle had not moved from her bench in front of the tavern.

21

The children were resting in a clearing ringed by tall trees. The sun was at its height. Kaourintin had told the older boys to take out the provisions they carried in their packs. Withénoc stood a little to one side, eating some bread and onions and watching the children. As was their habit, the younger boys and girls had gathered around Kaourintin, and now sat eating silently. The only ones talking were Goranton, Anna and some of the older children.

'Why are we still in the forest?' asked Anna. 'Could we not have taken the road? We should have reached Carhaix by now.'

The little dark-haired girl, dressed like a boy in breeches and a woollen tunic, looked confidently at the shepherd. She was from a wealthy family in Carhaix. Her quick wit, her determination and her faith had gained her much respect from her comrades. She had wanted to become a nun like her aunt, and when she heard Kaourintin preaching in the marketplace in Carhaix she had followed him without hesitation.

'I have already asked Withénoc this question, Anna,' said Kaourintin. 'It seems that Broérec's men are patrolling the roads. It is better to be prudent and stay hidden.'

'I have the impression,' said Goranton, 'that since leaving Lannédern we have been going round in a circle. Don't you think so?'

'No,' replied Kaourintin, looking daggers at him. 'Come, Goranton, I would like to speak with you on your own.'

The boy hesitated a moment but then followed his leader away from the group.

'What is it, Kaourintin? What do you have to say that the others should not hear?'

'Stop asking me questions,' said Kaourintin imperiously. 'You will needlessly upset the children.'

'But . . .'

'I am not a fool,' Kaourintin interrupted. 'I know we have been going round in circles all day. And I would like to know why, too, but I can't get a word out of Withénoc. We must keep our eyes open. Tell Anna. She has a good head on her shoulders and she will be useful. But we must on no account let the others know there is anything wrong. We are their guides, Goranton, and their lives are in our hands.'

'Especially you, Kaourintin. It is your crusade.'

'I know it only too well. But I need your help. You have always been a loyal companion, and Anna is a valiant girl. There are too many things I don't understand, Goranton.'

'What do you mean?'

'The children who disappeared from Saint-Herbot, With-énoc's attitude, and now this wandering around in the forest as though we are waiting for something. But what is that something? Careful, here he is. Tell Anna what I told you.'

The monk was walking towards them, his habit billowing around his ankles.

'We must leave, Kaourintin,' he said in his muted voice.

'But we have just got here. The little ones need more rest.'

'We shall be making a long stop soon, I promise you. But I think I heard barking in the distance. The woods are not safe, you know that.'

'I heard nothing,' retorted the shepherd. 'And it was you who told us we would be safe here. May I speak privately with you, Withénoc?'

'Another time. Give the order to leave, and follow me.'

He turned and walked off through the ferns without waiting for a reply. Kaourintin reluctantly told his little band to break camp and follow in Withénoc's footsteps.

Anna helped the smaller children with their packs and hurried them along so they could keep up with the rest. Goranton brought up the rear, relating his discussion with

Kaourintin to Anna as they walked. The girl nodded her head in agreement.

She too detested the monk. She had found him repulsive from the moment she laid eyes on him; he was like a spider in his black robe, with his arms that were much too long for his body and his way of moving so quickly that he could be next to you without you having seen him coming. And why did he never show his face, not even to Kaourintin? She had several times suggested that they leave without the monk but the shepherd said he needed the help of an adult. He did not know which roads to take to reach the Holy Land. He could not even imagine how far away it was. Withénoc had thus gained a hold over the boy, telling him of the various monasteries they could stop in on their way.

22

A man-at-arms stood waiting for Galeran when he arrived back at the château. The knight was instructed to join Broérec immediately in the upper room of the keep.

'Tell me,' Galeran said to the soldier, 'have you seen Drogon or Thustan?'

'I have not seen Thustan, but Drogon hasn't budged since he came back from the hunt.'

'Thank you. Please take my horse and give him some hay. But leave the saddle on.'

'Very well, sir,' said the soldier, leading Quolibet off to the stables.

Galeran found Broérec pacing up and down the room, overcome with the fear that misfortune had befallen the only son he loved.

'Well?' he cried when he saw Galeran.

'Calm yourself, Broérec! Let me sit down. I have not yet found any trace of your son. But I have learned many things of which you do not seem to be aware and which could be connected to Jestin's disappearance.'

The ringing of a bell interrupted the knight. Broérec froze, listening to the repeated calls of a horn. The sound of hurrying footsteps came from above.

'Follow me,' said Broérec, climbing the ladder to the top of the tower.

There was a wind blowing, but it was not strong enough to disperse the thick column of black smoke that rose above the forest.

'It's Cléophas's farm!' said one of the watchmen.

'I can see that, you clod,' growled Broérec. 'You over there, get me ten men, and fast!'

He turned to the knight, who stared intently at the smoke.

'No doubt about it,' Broérec said. 'It's Cléophas's place all right. Those damned peasants again! They don't dare attack the château so they have a go at the farm.'

'That would surprise me,' replied Galeran. 'They hold Dame Génovéfa in great esteem.'

The two men clambered back down the ladder and rushed out into the courtyard where they were soon joined by Drogon. Ten men-at-arms were busy getting the horses ready.

Cléophas came hurtling out of his kitchen.

'Sir Knight!' he cried in great distress. 'Sir Knight, save them, I beg you.'

Galeran, who had just mounted his steed, leaned down to speak with the poor man.

'Trust me,' he said, then rode off.

The drawbridge had been lowered and Galeran galloped out behind the soldiers. He spurred his horse on and soon caught up with Broérec and Drogon as they rode along the track that led to the farm. The acrid smell of smoke soon replaced the sweet odours of the forest. On the way they passed peasants running towards the fire. But when they got to the clearing Galeran knew it was already too late. Flames leaped from the buildings and the intense heat prevented anyone from approaching.

Broérec dismounted and ordered his men to tie their horses to some nearby trees. As he spoke, the roof of the farmhouse fell in with a terrible crash.

In the courtyard people from neighbouring hamlets rushed around, shouting orders which nobody obeyed. Some had cut long branches and were beating at the smaller flames on the ground. There were not enough buckets to make a chain to the cistern. The chaos increased as the fire spread.

The flames caught the thatch on the byre and the beasts inside cried out in fear. Galeran doused himself with water and ran through the thick clouds of smoke. But by the time he got the door of the building open it was too late – the cows were dead, suffocated by the black smoke. Broérec meanwhile looked for Dame Génovéfa and her son among the crowd of peasants, calling but finding no reply.

The fire raged on until nightfall and then died out, like an ogre who has eaten his fill. The peasants filed off into the forest. Broérec and Galeran sat on the ground and contemplated the smouldering ruins.

'It will be many hours before we can safely enter the house,' said Galeran. 'God knows what we shall find there.'

'Dame Génovéfa and her son might have managed to escape with their old servant woman,' ventured Broérec. 'I'll tell my men to search for them.'

'There were three farmhands as well,' said Drogon, who had emerged from the darkness.

He had helped the peasants with an ardour that astonished Galeran. He stood now in front of his father, his face blackened and sweat running down his brow.

'If I find the devils who did this . . .' he muttered.

'You think it was no accident?' asked Galeran.

But the young man had no time to reply, for at that moment a soldier came running up to them.

'Sirs! Sirs! Come, come!'

They followed him to the orchard, where they were confronted with the bloody body of Dame Génovéfa's old servant, which lay next to that of her young master. Génovéfa herself swung from a rope tied to an apple tree. Her blue dress was torn and covered with blood. Her face had been slashed and was barely recognisable. Her eyes were gouged and hung down over her cheeks. Yann and the servant had merely had their throats cut.

Galeran, sickened by the horror before him, looked at Génovéfa's twisted body and wondered what demon could have done such a vile deed.

'And to think she believed her silence would protect her!' he mused.

Broérec gave a terrible cry and ran towards the body to cut it down.

'Help me, Galeran,' he shouted. 'Catch her!'

The knight caught the body as it slid down the trunk and into his arms. He laid her down on the grass next to the other corpses. Broérec knelt down by her side and stroked her face.

'But why?' he said in a cold rage. 'And this poor boy! He was like a brother to Jestin.'

He beat his forehead with his clenched fists.

'Who did it? The peasants? That bastard Hoël? Robbers who tortured her to find out where she hid her money? The ones whose fires we see in the forest?'

'I think not,' said Galeran. 'You forget that the lookouts in the villages would have seen them coming.'

As he spoke, the knight looked around him and memorised every detail of the macabre scene: the grass trampled by what must have been several people, the fact that Génovéfa's gold chain was no longer around her neck, the wounds inflicted on each of the bodies . . .

'We can see roughly how this was done,' he said. 'The three of them were gathering apples when the killers arrived. They tried to flee. The old servant was the slowest and was the first to be caught and killed. Yann stood in front of his mother to protect her and became the second victim. But it was Géno-véfa that they were really after.'

'Why her?'

'She knew too many things, Broérec. She had too many secrets.'

'And do you think she told them anything?' the giant asked in a hushed voice.

'I may be wrong, but I think not. They made a mistake by killing her beloved son first. Her grief must have made her wish for her own death. They had no hold over her after that. I think the killers failed in their mission and took what vengeance they could by torching the farm.'

'What about the missing farmhands? It would not be the first time servants pillaged their master. Why look any further?'

'On the contrary, I think we must look much further, and that includes looking into your past,' murmured the knight under his breath.

Drogon had remained silent during this conversation. Galeran now glanced at him, then turned away again. He knelt down and covered Génovéfa with his cloak.

'Let us bring these three back to the château,' said Broérec. 'And now I must find out what has become of Jestin!'

Galeran, for his part, was thinking of Cléophas. How would he take this latest blow? Would he, like Job, lament the day he was born and the night his son was conceived?

Four men-at-arms were ordered to stay and guard what was left of the farm. The victims were placed on improvised stretchers and carried off towards the château by the rest of the soldiers.

23

The journey seemed interminable to Galeran, who was over-whelmed more by disgust than fatigue. Drogon rode at the head of the party, apparently indifferent to his surroundings. The only sign that he was troubled was the pallor of his face. Broérec was even paler than his son, and stopped several times to vomit. Galeran took up the rear, turning often to look behind him; he thought he could see a furtive figure following the group.

At last they arrived at the château, and the knight braced himself for the moment when old Cléophas would have to be told the news. Men-at-arms stood in the courtyard await-ing their comrades' return and bombarding them with ques-tions as they dismounted. Broérec and Drogon ignored them and went straight into the keep.

Galeran asked after the cook. Titik, his assistant, came forward.

'He is in the stables, sir.'

'What is he doing there?'

'Sleeping!'

'What!' said the knight, who felt somehow relieved.

'He's drunk,' said the boy, with a faint smile on his lips.

Around them the soldiers stood and waited for orders. Galeran told them to carry the bodies to the cellar. He himself took Yann's corpse and brought it to where he had laid little Fanchon. He noticed that the millstone was still and that the wretch who had turned it was no longer there.

'Tell me, boy,' he said to Titik. 'Where is the fellow who turned the stone?'

'Gone, sir.'

'You mean dead?'

'No. Lord Broérec told him that was enough and chased him out.'

'When was that?'

'Yesterday.'

It then occurred to the knight that when he was eating with Cléophas the previous night he had not heard the grinding of the millstone.

'Do you know who he was?'

'He wasn't from around here,' Titik replied cagily.

'Boy, I am going to charge you with a very important message. You are used to delivering messages, are you not?'

'I am, sir.'

'Good. You must go to Saint-Herbot and seek out Gweltaz Ar Fur. Tell him what has happened and ask him to send some women to prepare the bodies for burial. You must also bring Père Gwen to pray for them and find them some consecrated ground where they may be laid to rest.'

Broérec sat at the table before a goblet of his foul liquor. He muttered to himself and gritted his teeth. Galeran placed a hand on his shoulder.

'Broérec,' he said softly, 'stop tormenting yourself. I swear to you before God that nothing bad has happened to Jestin and that you will see him soon.'

'It is a dark and black world we live in,' said the giant, staring into space.

Tears rolled down his weathered face. Galeran, seeing that nothing could draw him out of his misery, withdrew to his room to take stock of events.

24

He sat on the bed and placed on his lap a wax tablet. In his hand he held a stylus. He loved this ancient method of making notes that could so easily be erased. On the tablet he traced a maze. It was not the holy maze that believers followed on their knees to reach Jerusalem, but a labyrinth that led to the place where the damned were tortured. But who was the Minotaur crouching at the end of the maze? And how could the land be delivered from his murderous folly?

Galeran marked a series of points representing the château, the farm, the hamlets. He marked also the circular route the children had taken, as well as the tracks the hunt had followed. Then he took another tablet and wrote down his questions.

Who had really paid Broérec's ransom? How could he have paid his men at Vitré when he had just this miserable fief to support him? Why was Dame Génovéfa tortured? Why did she stay at the farm instead of going back to live in comfort and security in Normandy? Was Cléophas merely an indulgent husband?

Then he placed the two tablets on the ground before him. His eyes jumped around the tortuous labyrinth and suddenly everything became clear to him.

25

Hoël the bastard now never left Ninian's refuge. He wondered if he had not been bewitched by the meandering underground river and the transparent lake.

Today, while the sky outside was still coloured with smoke from the fire at Génovéfa's farm, Hoël and Ninian amused themselves by watching some crayfish that hovered hesitantly around a piece of bait. They would hoist one out of the water from time to time, causing the others to flee to hiding places under stones by the bank. Hoël would throw a tiny piece of meat into the pool and they would come rushing back again, to the great delight of the young pair.

Ninian suddenly gave a little cry – a large crayfish had nipped her finger. She grabbed the creature and flung it far out into the lake, then sucked the pinch mark.

'Did it pinch you hard? I hate it when you are hurt!' said Hoël.

'Don't be silly. It's nothing.'

They fell silent for a while, for their game had lost its sparkle.

'Tell me, Ninian,' Hoël said suddenly, 'why don't you want to go back to your father? You can't stay here for ever. The fine weather will be over soon and I can tell you, it's not pleasant being outdoors in the winter.'

The girl's eyes filled with tears and she turned her face away.

'I don't want to go back there and take part in that awful business any more. And there's that beast Drogon – he hates me because our father makes such a fuss over me and does whatever I ask. I know he's watching me. If he ever finds out who I really am and tells Broérec . . . My father would simply throw me out!'

'Why don't you go to Génovéfa's farm then? She would look after you. She brought you up, after all.'

'I haven't been to the farm for months,' said Ninian, shrugging her shoulders.

'Why not?'

'It's Yann,' she sighed. 'I wonder if his mother hasn't told him the truth about me. But whatever the reason, he's always giving me strange looks.'

'Don't worry about that. In any case, you're well able to defend yourself. That I know!'

'Perhaps. But that's not all. Do you know what I saw one day as I arrived at the farm?'

'How should I know?'

'Well, I saw Drogon leaving. And he looked well pleased with himself.'

'Drogon?'

'And that came as a great shock to me, for I've always had great trust in Dame Génovéfa. What she said I took as gospel. She told me she could not bear Drogon and would throw him out if ever he ventured to the farm. And suddenly I see the pig at her house, and smiling to himself as he walks away.'

She paused to shake her head in disgust.

'I decided to watch the farm, and saw Drogon going there several times and each time leaving with a satisfied look on his face. So, for me, the farm now belongs to the past.'

'If that's the case, then I think you are right not to go there,' said Hoël.

'When I think of it!' cried Ninian bitterly. 'Génovéfa, whom I loved like my mother, and there she was in league with that beast.'

'Don't get upset, Ninian. If that's the case, then Drogon must know about you now. I wonder what he's plotting with Génovéfa, but I'm sure it's nothing good.'

'Exactly. that's why I ran away. I realised that if Drogon wanted to attack me, he could easily do so at the farm with the blessing of that traitress. They would leave my body in the forest where the wolves would devour it. And then it would be said that I had disappeared just like the children.'

'Stop, Ninian! Don't speak like that.'

'But it's the truth.'

'Do you know, Ninian, why I shoot my arrows at that ignoble Thustan and why I attack Broérec's men? It's because I do not wish to live like a hunted animal. It's easy for ten men to hunt a single beast or a woman. And for them there's no difference. That's how they treated my mother. But I'm a hunter too, and I don't need a pack of hounds. Anyone who threatens you, Ninian, will have to deal with me.'

'What do you plan to do?'

'Exactly what I've been doing all these years. I'll track them down. Wherever they go, whenever they think they are the first there, I shall always have been there before them.'

'Yet you did not see Drogon at Génovéfa's.'

'True, but I did spot him somewhere else. And that was a sight worth seeing, I tell you! But what do you think of that knight who has been living at the château?'

'I don't know what to make of him. But he sticks his nose in everywhere and I don't like that. He's meant to be a friend of my father's – if Broérec is capable of having friends.'

'I have spoken with him and he seems to me a man you can trust.'

She cast him a sidelong glance and shrugged her shoulders.

'You men are all the same. You admire him because he's tall and strong and has a horse and fine weapons.'

Hoël looked at her sullenly. When he spoke again he avoided her eye.

'Ninian, why do you not love me?'

'Oh Hoël, don't bore me with that again. Please!'

'But I love you, Ninian,' he said, still not looking at her. 'I want you to become my lady.'

She turned to face him, her cheeks suddenly scarlet.

'You are mad! Who put that idea into your head?'

'But I have heard that kings marry their sisters.'

'That is not true! Or if it is then it was the Turks. Let me tell you another story that I learned from Père Gwen. On the Rhine, or perhaps even in Denmark – no matter where – a prince married his cousin because he loved her more than anything else in the world. The Pope excommunicated the pair of them. Then they took a vow of chastity and as penance set off with the Crusaders for the Holy Land. They died there and were placed in the same tomb. And that wasn't even his sister, it was his cousin!'

'But Ninian, that's a wonderful story. I would like to do as they did.'

'Well, I wouldn't,' the girl replied severely.

He looked at her, infinite sadness in his eyes. She returned his gaze, then suddenly flung her arms around him and began crying, her head buried in his broad shoulders.

PART FOUR

La bête va bondir . . .
Temps de tempêtes, temps des loups.
Avant que le monde s'effondre,
Personne n'épargnera personne.

The beast will spring . . .
In the hour of the storm, the hour of the wolf.
When the world is about to fall apart,
No man will spare another.

From the Scandinavian poem *Volüpsa*

26

The next morning Galeran decided to return alone to the farm. There he found the four soldiers whom Broérec had posted sitting around a fire eating a rabbit they had just cooked.

'I greet you, men. How was your night here? Did anybody come?'

'No, Sir Galeran,' came the reply from the oldest of the four.

'Except Thustan,' said another.

'And what did he want?'

'He said he was looking for Lord Broérec. He had a good look around but he didn't go near the buildings because they were still smoking. And then off he went.'

'Is it safe to visit the buildings now?'

'We've not been in yet. But there was a shower earlier, so it should be all right. We have to remove the carcasses of those poor beasts that were burned to death.'

Galeran glanced around him. A weak sun meanly lit the ruins of this once prosperous farmstead. The smell of damp ashes filled the air. The fire had completely destroyed the roof, but the old stone walls had held up and he was able to enter the house with little difficulty. There was no trace of furniture in the room where he had shared a drink with Dame Génovéfa. Only the stone hearth remained intact.

'So it was not here that the fire took hold,' he murmured to himself. 'And what is this?'

Some of the flagging had caved in under the intense heat. Galeran peered into the hole and saw that there was a large crypt or cellar there. Its walls were smooth and very old. He climbed down into it and realised immediately that he was in a hypocaust, a Roman heating system in which hot air circulated under the floor and between double walls. Like the old drainage systems, they were still capable of functioning perfectly despite having been abandoned for centuries.

But the place in which he now found himself had evidently been used for other purposes. He moved forward and found what was left of two ancient fireclay ovens. Next to them, half buried under a pile of broken flagstones, stood a little pyramid of ingots. He picked one up, sniffed it, scratched it with his nail, rubbed it on his tunic and then hurried back out of the building.

The men-at-arms were still gathered around the fire.

'We haven't slept all night, sir,' said the oldest. 'There's too much misfortune here. The Devil must have come out of the Yeûn and is amusing himself.'

'Perhaps you are right,' replied Galeran, considering the man. 'I believe Dame Génovéfa led a very quiet life here.'

He had often noted that a false declaration could procure more information than a direct question, and now his ploy was successful once again.

'Not everyone would say that, sir,' protested the soldier.

'I am not from these parts and am merely repeating what I have heard in the village. The people there held Dame Génovéfa in great esteem, for she did many good things for them.'

'You believe what those dogs tell you?'

'And why not?'

'You would do well to watch out. Did you not think that if they say she is good, then there might be reasons for that?'

Galeran did not reply. He waited for the man to go on, but he said no more. Instead he went back to chewing on his rabbit.

The knight, deciding not to push the matter, walked over to Quolibet, jumped into his saddle and galloped off. He knew now what he had to do.

27

Titik was alone in the kitchen.

'Where is Cléophas?' asked Galeran as he entered the room.

'He went to see the bodies and then he left. He didn't say where for, but I think he has gone to the farm.'

'I have just come from there, yet I did not see him. Have you done what I asked?'

'I have. The women are with the dead and Père Gwen shouldn't be long.'

'What about the others? Are they upstairs?'

'Yes. I've just brought Broérec and Drogon some broth, but Jestin is not back yet.'

'Thank you, Titik,' said the knight, handing the boy a coin.

'I cannot take it, sir. I would be profiting from the dead, and that would bring bad luck. And besides, I was Fanchon's betrothed, and only you will be able to find out who killed her.'

The boy's trust inspired Galeran. The child walked up to him and took his hand briefly before returning to the oven. The knight opened his fist and found a small piece of parchment bearing a message written in a clumsy hand. Titik stared at him as he read the text. He nodded, then handed back the parchment.

'Here, throw that in the fire,' he said with a smile.

Broérec was alone in the upper room. He sat there lapping his soup as Galeran climbed the ladder and walked past as though he had not seen him. The knight went to his room and returned bearing the fur that Broérec had given him to keep him warm at night. He threw it on the table in front of the giant, then went back to his room where he began to pack his belongings. Broérec watched him, his mouth hanging open in astonishment. He got up and went to the door of the knight's room.

'And what does this mean?'

'Guess,' said Galeran, glancing up at him.

'By God, you're not leaving me, are you?'

'For once, Broérec, you're right.'

'But why?' cried the giant. 'And what about Jestin?'

'Broérec, do you really think I am stupid?'

'When did I ever say that?' groaned Broérec, who now showed no trace of his usual self-assurance. 'Stay, Galeran, I beg you.'

Galeran burst into laughter.

'Perhaps I will,' he said. 'But it depends.'

'On what?'

'On what you are about to tell me.'

At this Broérec lowered his eyes and sat back down again at the table. Galeran pulled up a stool and sat next to him. From his tunic he took the ingot he had found in the farmhouse and placed it on the table.

'What do you say to that, Broérec?'

'I say . . . I say . . . It's a piece of silver.'

The knight got up to leave.

'No! No! Stay, Galeran. I swear to you I do not know anything. Wait here, I want to show you something.'

He jumped up from the table and ran to his box bed, into which he disappeared, slamming the shutters behind him. Galeran heard a creaking noise and the giant re-emerged with an ingot in his hand. He put it down on the table. It was longer than Galeran's and a little tarnished, and a stamp mark was visible on its surface. The knight took it in his hand to feel its weight.

'That is what you paid your ransome at Vitré with, is it not? You never did get into debt, and Tanguy never gave you a penny to have you released!'

'It is true,' said Broérec. 'But how did you guess?'

'I didn't guess anything. You told me.'

'What do you mean, I told you?'

'I saw the number of men you have here, and the poverty of your fief. A man cannot have a garrison as well equipped as yours, nor make war for ten years, if his hired soldiers are not paid handsomely. As you yourself reminded me the other day, mercenaries never fight for the sake of honour. So I knew you had to have other resources. I found this ingot at the farm.'

'At the farm?' said Broérec, turning the piece of metal over in his hand. 'At Dame Génovéfa's place? But it has just been cast. And look, it's a different size to mine.'

There was a silence as the two men considered each other.

'Listen, Broérec,' Galeran finally said, 'tell me about your father's death. Who found him in the forest?'

'I did. He had fallen from his horse but was not yet dead.'

'No, but he was dying, his face black and half blind . . . He too was poisoned!'

'But it was not I who did it! I never killed my father!'

'I know. Your father died from his excesses.'

'How can you know such a thing?'

Galeran laughed.

'That vexes you, does it not? You sent for me, thinking you were so clever you could use me. But you should have remembered Vitré. How many times did we play that game with coins?'

'And you won every time!' groaned the giant.

'That's right. Do you remember, one player would have a certain number of coins in his closed fist and the other would have to guess how many there were. It is supposed to be a game of chance, but with practice one can come to guess correctly almost every time. So, Broérec, you can open up your hand now, I know what you have in there.'

'Very well,' said Broérec with a grimace. 'You are not mistaken, and may the Devil . . .'

'Leave the Devil out of this and speak.'

'The mine does exist. It dates back to the time of the

Romans, perhaps even beyond then. But it was forgotten about for a long time and bramble bushes covered it up. My father came across the entrance one day when he was chasing a stag. He went in and found everything more or less intact, apart from the struts of some of the walls that had collapsed. The last people to use the mine, the Romans or the Celts or whoever they were, must have left in a hurry, for there was a pile of ingots ready to be carried away sitting at the entrance. My father saw this, and immediately killed the two trackers who accompanied him. The old man's head was never that solid but I think the discovery was the last straw for him. He spent his time there counting and recounting the ingots, or scratching around to see if he couldn't find more.'

'He could have reopened the mine,' ventured Galeran.

'He didn't want to. It was his secret, and he was afraid of being robbed. He only told me about it when I found him dying in the forest. He asked me to tell his sins to Père Gwen so he might gain absolution for his crimes.'

'And you did that for him?'

'You jest?' said Broérec with a terrifying smile.

'So you are responsible for your own father's eternal damnation? And does that not keep you awake at night?'

Broérec did not respond. He sat silently as Galeran stared at him.

'Very well,' said the knight, 'let us now speak of you.'

'I saw it as an opportunity to equip my men-at-arms and go off to do battle, as I had long desired. So I rolled a few stones over the entrance to the mine and took the ingots back to the château and hid them. There was enough to keep me happy.'

'But there was still so much silver to be mined there,' said Galeran, gesturing towards the ingot he had placed on the table.

'I know, I know,' replied Broérec. 'But I thought about how costly a business it is to work a mine. I did consider it, especially when my good lady was still here. In fact, Mechtilde encouraged me. She told me about seams of lead they found in the Harz mountains that contained silver and that made the people there very rich. She even suggested that I get miners from there to work here.'

'I've heard that Germanic miners work in mines as far away as Wales,' replied Galeran. 'They are renowned for their expertise and skill.'

'But I decided in the end not to do anything. I would have had to pay them far too much. I reckoned I would lose more than I would gain.'

'I see. Tell me, do you often go up to the top of the keep?'

'From time to time, particularly if there is an alert. But it is mostly Drogon who goes there, since he is in charge of the men-at-arms. He's up there at the moment, in fact.'

'Then that is where we must go,' said the knight, jumping to his feet. 'We don't have much time.'

A dumbfounded Broérec followed him up the ladder.

28

The morning was already well advanced. The sombre silhouette of Menez Mikêl cut through the vivid blue of the sky. Crows circled above the keep. But Galeran, leaning out over the parapet, paid them no attention. He was staring out into the distance, observing a thin plume of smoke that hung above the trees.

Drogon had said it was smoke from hunters' fires. Yet it burned day and night. The knight instinctively knew it marked the position of the silver mine. He pointed at it as he spoke to Broérec.

'We must go there.'

'It's true that the fire is in the direction of the old mine, but that doesn't mean anything. No one would have dared start working it again. They would have to deal with flooding, with cave-ins, with all those overgrown bushes and brambles. No, I am sure that is nothing more than a poacher's fire.'

'Do you know many poachers who give away their position by having a fire going night and day?' retorted Galeran.

Drogon came to Broérec's defence.

'Father is right. When we went there with the dogs we found nothing but the remains of a fire made by hunters. The dogs were afraid to go any further into the rocks – it's a place for wolves, not men.'

Galeran turned and looked the young man straight in the eye.

'That is also what I think, Drogon. Do you know where the mine is?'

Drogon hesitated.

'You do,' said Broérec. 'Remember, I brought you there a few years ago with Jestin. I wanted you to get to know your domain in case I did not return from Vitré. It's roughly at the spot where we can see that smoke now.'

'Ah yes, I think I recall going there,' said Drogon. 'But it looked like just another pile of rocks to me.'

'Enough of this idle talk,' growled Broérec. 'Let us go there now and I shall deal with these poachers.'

At this point Drogon asked if he might be excused.

'But my son,' retorted Broérec, 'we need you, and your dogs! You must come with us. Tell a dozen of the men to stand ready. We shall quickly put an end to these devilish marauders.'

Without a word, Drogon turned and climbed down the ladder. His father watched him as he went.

'Are you content now?' he asked Galeran. 'At least now we shall clear up this particular matter.'

The knight nodded sombrely.

'Can you not take more soldiers with you? I think, Broérec, that we may well come across stiffer opposition than you think.'

'You're mad! These folk will not know how to fight, and anyway I cannot withdraw any more men from the château. Especially now after the fire at the farm. If these poachers want war, they shall have it. I do not fear them.'

'Why do you insist on believing this poacher story? It is made up simply to scare off the curious, just like the tale of the giant wolves. Have you already forgotten what I brought you back from the farm? We both know that the ingot did not come from your own stock. The mould was not the same. So? Do you think that Génovéfa had a sufficiently large fortune to have a pile of ingots in her cellar?'

'Very well. I concede.'

'What is the place like?'

'There is a rocky hill and a valley with cliffs on both sides. But after Vitré we are well used to that sort of terrain. And I am on home territory here, do not forget that!'

Galeran gave him a vague smile. He was thinking that there

139

were many aspects of this sinister business that would come as a decidedly unpleasant surprise to his old comrade-in-arms.

'Then we must hope your local knowledge will give us an advantage. Let us meet in the stables. I want to see to my horse and also to find out if Cléophas is back yet.'

'I have not seen him this morning.'

'Titik says he kept watch over the bodies and then left for the farm at dawn.'

'Do you think he knows about the ingots?'

'I don't know, Broérec. But let us hurry, we have lost enough time and the day is getting on.'

With that they descended the ladders. Galeran went first to his room, from where he looked through the loophole to see Broérec cross the yard and enter the stables. The soldiers scurried around, harried by Drogon's harsh words, leaving their javelins and bows against the palisade as they pulled on their coats of mail.

'Now things will come to a head,' thought the knight.

He put on his own coat of mail and over it his cloak. He loved the ceremony of these preparations. He tied his belt, slipped his dagger into its leather sheath, and felt rise within him the exhilaration that precedes battle, the excitement that comes from knowing this may be one's last day on earth.

Finally, he took his sword and left his room, pulling the door shut behind him.

29

Water, green from the saltpetre that lined the sides of the vast underground cavern, streamed down the walls. The only light came from a torch that was about to burn itself out. It was very cold. The children slept a troubled sleep, piled next to each other like baby animals on the straw-covered floor. Today, because one of the galleries had collapsed, they had been allowed to sleep longer than usual.

A heavy step from a nearby tunnel awoke some of them. It was mealtime. The youngest slept on, exhausted, until their companions shook them out of their uneasy dreams. The man who now arrived in the room was a sturdy fellow dressed in a leather tunic and breeches. He pulled behind him a cart on which stood a large steaming pot.

When he opened the grille that held the children in their dormitory most of them had already risen shakily to their feet. They were a pitiful group, with their ragged clothes, their emaciated bodies and their bowls stretched out before them.

The man paid no attention to their miserable state. Every morning he brought them their first meal of the day, a disgusting cereal mush whose only merit was that it was almost hot. The cook, on his generous days, threw in a few bones, over which the children would squabble. Indeed, despite the horrible smell of the food, the hungry prisoners would always push and elbow each other to get their fair share.

Suddenly one of the boys dropped his bowl with a groan and fell to the ground. He began vomiting, and his head hit the floor repeatedly as he scratched the earth.

The gaoler watched for a moment, then walked over and grabbed the child by the hair. He lifted his face, saw the bulging eyes, the convulsions, the vomit, and seemed satisfied. He told two horrified boys to pick up the patient and to follow him. His strict orders were that the sick must immediately be segregated from the others.

Some of the children who fell ill would be contorted with pain before losing their reason, while others would suffer dreadfully from vomiting and diarrhoea, or would be paralysed. But whatever their symptoms, death was always the result.

A special room had been set aside for the sick at the other end of the underground complex. In reality it was a place for them to die, for no child ever left it alive. From the room came groans and cries like those of wounded animals, then a heavy silence would follow.

The tunnel was so narrow that the girl could advance only on all fours. Torches placed at intervals lit the glinting walls of the mine. Mônik moved slowly, bracing herself against the block of stone which was attached by a thick rope to her waist. She could hear the panting breath of the girl who followed behind her, burdened too with a heavy load.

Large icy drops of water seeping through the roof fell on her neck and ran down her shoulders onto her worn tunic. Pain spread up from her chafed knees and into her lower back. She slipped on a wet flagstone and landed with a thump on her elbow. She stopped for a moment to gather herself and to try to overcome the weariness and cold that permeated her body. She tried to wipe away the blood that stained her limbs, then quickly began to heave the rock forward again – she feared she would be whipped if she delayed any further.

She quickly caught up with the small boy in front of her. He was little more than skin and bones, and coughed incessantly. Mônik knew he was not much longer for this world. In the short time she had been in this place she had come to understand that the incomprehensible evil at work here would soon take her too. She would end up in the room at the end of the tunnel, the 'tomb' as the children called it, and her body would later be flung into a pit with the other corpses.

Mônik, or Little Môn as her parents called her, hailed from Braspartz. She was a lively and spirited girl. Just a few days before she had created a diversion to help Kadou escape by plunging into the river. Now she hoped and prayed to the Virgin that he would soon return. Each day she dreamed of seeing him walk into the tunnel with men of her village who would deliver her from this hell that was worse than anything the priest of Braspartz had ever depicted in his sermons.

What she did not know was that the malady had already taken root in Kadou before he left, and that his lifeless form lay next to Fanchon's in the cemetery at Lannédern.

There were ten of them working in the gallery. Ten of them trudging through the icy mud, breaking rocks and hauling stone to be sorted by men who waited with whips. Most of the tunnels were so cramped that even a small adult would not have been able to pass through them. Only children could be used to extract the precious ore.

Mônik had noted that the boys who worked in the gallery did not live long. They would die of exhaustion or would be taken by the malady more quickly than the others. With heavy picks they created showers of sparks as they cut out big chunks of grey galena. A fine silver dust shimmered in the air and cut the children's throats as it filled up their lungs. At the far end of the gallery the air grew thicker, making breathing difficult and work even more fatiguing.

In total, there were forty children and fifteen adults in the mine. The children who worked in the forest, gathering wood for the furnaces, were less affected by the malady.

The sombre silhouette of the provisioner would arrive once a month at the mine entrance, escorted by a few fearful children he had rounded up. The gaolers would select the more robust to work at the rock face, but nevertheless the work advanced slowly. Much too slowly for the head man at the mine, who instructed his underlings to make free use of their whips.

This was how Fanchon had come to be punished, for she had dared to stop in the tunnel to rest a while and let the child behind her go ahead. The guard at the end of the tunnel spotted this, and gave her twenty lashes to teach her a lesson and to warn the other children not to slack. The punishment was so severe that it hastened the death of the already sick girl.

The gaolers had thought of enlarging the tunnels so that men could work there, but in the end decided that this would take too long. Besides, it was much easier to keep children in line, they ate less than adults and, if kept in a state of constant fear, could achieve considerable results.

Just three months before, they had come upon a rich seam of galena. The head man decided to bring in more children to speed up its extraction. The provisioner was due to arrive at any moment, and the rumour spread among the children that twenty new recruits were about to join them.

Since the new vein had been discovered the furnaces blazed night and day, and the underground spaces glowed red.

Mônik emerged from the tunnel and, slowly and painfully, straightened her back. The torches of the large room made her blink, for the longer she spent underground, the less could she bear the light. A boy came up to her and untied the rope from the rock she had dragged here. He gave her a little sign with his hand. Mônik nodded in response, coiled the rope around her slender waist and disappeared back down the tunnel.

The children had learned to communicate by signs. The only places where they could exchange a few words were the tunnels where adults could not enter.

Two older boys loaded the block Mônik had brought onto a litter and carried it out towards the light of day. Outside, on the platform overlooking the valley, men sorted the ore which would go to the foundry. When this was done, boys would carry it down to the river where two guards would go at it with large hammers. It was then sifted several times, washed and put back on the litter to be carried off to the furnace.

Hidden in one of the underground spaces was the foundry, an enormous brick construction topped by a strange metal dome, pierced by two holes where the workers could insert the bellows; a system of chains and pulleys enabled this huge lid to be opened in order to feed in more ore. Beneath it was a large pit, in which a fire blazed night and day. Thick black smoke escaped through a natural chimney.

For three days now they had been working the foundry feverishly. The two men in charge first placed the galena on the bed of bricks that was covered by a layer of ash and a layer of straw. Then they gently heated the ore for four hours until the litharge rose up. As soon as it began to do so, they stirred up the fire and got to work with bellows, sending cold air over the oxidising surface. Once all the litharge had been cleared, the molten lead began to flow along a channel in the base of the furnace. The men then closed the lid, making the temperature rise. Children rushed back and forth, carrying buckets of water which they placed near the furnace, and the men plunged their pincers into the molten metal.

The lead had been flowing for almost fifty hours now. The channel had to be cleaned from time to time to prevent blockages.

Lead ingots were piled to one side. But the two workers, like alchemists, seemed to be waiting for something else. They worked the pulleys to open the lid and examined the grey surface of the molten lead, heedless of the terrible vapours that rose up.

Suddenly there was a white flash in the bottom of the furnace. It sparked frenetic activity among the workers. They began shouting out orders and the children began to throw the buckets of water over the metal, which quickly filled the room with a thick cloud of vapour.

When this had dissipated a large disc of shiny, pure silver lay at the bottom of the furnace.

The men cried out in joy, for the harvest was a good one.

The galena was rich and the lead extracted from it was of excellent quality. Once shaped it could be sold for a good price to the merchants of Carhaix, who would then sell it on in Anjou or Aquitaine.

30

They had spent the night in a clearing. Withénoc woke them at dawn, and within minutes was leading them into a valley through which flowed one of the tributaries of the Elez. The place was wild and desolate. But smoke rose from a platform that overlooked the valley, and the sound of voices echoed over the rocky hillsides. By the time Kaourintin realised what was happening, it was too late.

A group of men sprang out from behind rocks and encircled the children, brutes with hard eyes and rough, hairy faces. The terrified children gathered around the shepherd boy, who stared fearfully at the men and their whips and sticks. Not knowing what to do, he turned to the monk.

With a brusque gesture Withénoc threw back his hood and at last showed his face to Kaourintin. He had abandoned his disguise to reveal himself as the slave merchant that he was, the man who each month delivered a new batch of children to the mine.

Kaourintin shivered at the sight. Ugly was too good a word to describe the man. Withénoc's skin was smooth and devoid of expression. There was darkness, or rather an absence of colour, in the deep well of his eyes.

Kaourintin was about to shout to the children to run when Withénoc grabbed him and held a knife to his neck.

'If anyone moves I shall slit his throat!' cried the monk.

His voice was calm and controlled. But the children heard in it a note of impatience and they knew he would carry out his threat if provoked. Anna, who had taken one of the smaller children's hands, began to back slowly away. Goranton watched Kaourintin's white face.

'Tell them not to move if you want to live,' the monk hissed at Kaourintin.

Thoughts raced through the boy's mind. If he told the children to run, it was likely that at least some of them would manage to escape.

'Why do you think I fear going to join Our Lord?' he asked in a low, calm voice.

Then he shouted.

'Run! Run, for they will kill us anyway.'

The monk pushed the point of his blade into Kaourintin's neck, and a trickle of blood emerged. The boy tried vainly to wriggle free, but Withénoc's grip was tight and he stood ready to plunge his knife deeper into his captive's skin.

'Stop!' came a cry from Goranton. 'We will not move, I swear to you!'

'It's lucky they are more reasonable than you,' said Withénoc, withdrawing his blade and throwing Kaourintin to the ground.

Anna ran to the boy and helped him to his feet. He coughed, and a trickle of blood flowed between his lips. She tore a strip from her smock and tied it around his neck. Kaourintin leaned on her for support. His head was spinning. He forced himself to take long, slow breaths to try to ignore the biting pain in his neck.

'What have you got in store for us, Withénoc?' he asked in a croaking voice.

'I have nothing in store for you. My time among you is over.'

'So you are behind the disappearances? I thought you might be, but I couldn't believe it. Not a monk, I told myself.'

'You are but a child, Kaourintin. And an imbecile. I am no more a monk than you are a bishop!'

'From your manner I could have sworn you were a monk,' persisted Kaourintin, ignoring the man's taunts. 'Who are you, then?'

'You are not entirely wrong. I was once a monk, a very long time ago. But that is of no importance. We go our separate ways here. I have kept my promise to you, for I have brought you to a new world. You have arrived in the Promised Land, my boy!'

'You are right,' murmured the shepherd, 'I am an imbecile. I let myself be taken in and, what is worse, I dragged these innocents along with me.'

'What's that you are saying?' asked the monk, who had not heard the boy's muttered words.

'What is this place, Withénoc? Is this where Fanchon died? And Janik's sons? Are they dead too?'

'Calm yourself, boy. You will soon be reunited with Janik's sons – if they are still alive – and with all the other children who "deserted" you.'

The guards had already begun their selection, sorting the strong from the weak. A girl screamed when one of the men forced her away from her little brother.

'Withénoc, stop this, I beg you!' shouted Kaourintin.

'What a fool you are, Kaourintin. To me you represent nothing more than a few extra coins in my pocket.'

With that he gave the boy a shove that sent him sprawling at the feet of one of the guards. Kaourintin got up, looked at the monk one last time, and turned to follow the line of children that was marching towards the mine.

31

Broérec and his men had ridden several leagues through the forest. They slowed their pace only when they had to go around a fallen tree trunk that blocked the path. Thustan galloped a little behind the others, next to Broérec and Drogon. The dogs ran silently, easily outpacing the horses.

Only Quolibet, his neck covered in sweat, could keep up with the hounds. He sensed that battle was near. Galeran loosened the bridle, knowing from experience that this would make his horse more agile. The two old comrades formed one body. The knight recalled the many occasions on which his steed had, by his skill and agility, saved him from mortal blows.

Drogon, lashing furiously at his mount, caught up with Galeran and made a sign for him to slow down. They had arrived at a rocky hill, and when Broérec came alongside them he held up his hand, ordering the men to halt.

'And I thought your horse was worthless!' he panted, pushing his horse alongside the knight.

'He's like his master,' said Galeran, stroking the beast's neck. 'He knows how to mislead everyone. The wind is against us, but that is a good thing, for it makes it less likely they will hear us. Are we far from the mine?'

'It's just behind that hill. There is a little gorge with a stream at the bottom. The waste water from the mine flows in there. Or at least it used to. The channels are probably blocked now. From this valley we can get to the platform that leads into the mine.'

'You mean we must go through the gorge? That would give us very little hope of escape if they are waiting for us. Is there not a way to approach it from above, by following the top of the cliff?'

'If they are indeed waiting for us, then that way would be worse. There is no cover on the top of the hill, so they would easily spot us.'

'So what do you suggest?'

'First, we should leave the horses here,' said Broérec, leaping from his saddle. 'It will take a good fifteen minutes' walk to get to the start of the gorge. Thustan, bring me the bag I prepared.'

Thustan brought him a large cloth bag which he immediately cut open.

'Here,' he said, handing Galeran a strip of dirty grey cloth. 'We took what we could, we had to work fast.'

The knight seized the strip Broérec handed him, then took a second. The other men followed suit. Whey they had all wrapped their boots in the cloth, Broérec gave the signal for them to start. The Lord of Huelgoat had taken charge of operations. Drogon stayed at the rear, obediently following his father's instructions. This reversal of the usual order of things was not lost on Broérec, who smiled as he considered it.

'Let us go! You there, you stay with the horses. Come on, men.'

Broérec had taken on the authoritative air he had last displayed when setting out on patrol from Vitré. He was once again becoming the old warrior Galeran had known many years before. The knight much preferred this version of the man.

The men made their way around a pile of fallen rocks and found themselves at the entrance to a long gully with very steep, rocky sides. Through it flowed a stream, bordered by a pebbly bank. The place was strangely silent. The further they penetrated, the more Galeran was convinced that this was an ideal place for an ambush. The group made little noise as it advanced, but the knight knew that a good lookout would certainly hear or spot them. It also struck him that since they had entered the valley they had seen not a single bird.

151

The silence grew heavier. The only sounds to be heard were the crunch of their feet on the pebbles and the rattle of the swords that hung at their sides. A ray of sun found its way into the gorge and made the stream sparkle, momentarily dazzling them.

The place would have been idyllic were it not for the possibility that it could at any moment turn into a slaughterhouse, thought Galeran. He gripped the handle of his sword, and turned to check on Thustan and Drogon, who were bringing up the rear.

It was at this precise moment that the attack began. The knight heard a low rumble, then saw heavy rocks tumbling down the hillside behind them. A volley of arrows flew down at them from a clifftop.

'Get behind those rocks!' roared Galeran, pointing to a spot to their right.

His warning came too late for two of their number, who were hit and had to be dragged to cover. The men cowered between the rocks and the cliff, scanning the heights for signs of their enemy. But there was nothing to be seen, and no more arrows came.

Galeran, kneeling by a rock a little apart from the others, thought the sudden silence ominous. He looked behind him and saw that the rocks that had been pushed down the cliff now formed an effective barrier that blocked any chance of escape in that direction.

'Galeran!' came Broérec's voice. 'Galeran, come over here.'

The knight glanced around him, then ran, bent double, over to the giant. He crouched beside him, throwing back his hood and shaking the dust from it.

'What do you think?' asked Broérec.

'It doesn't look promising. As we might have expected. Is it far to the mine entrance?'

'No. We are very close, but you cannot see it because of the bushses. If we . . .'

'Give yourselves up and no harm will come to you!' bellowed a voice that Galeran thought he recognised.

'Go to . . .' Broérec began, but the knight stopped him.

'Remember Vitré,' Galeran said to him with a smile. 'We gave ourselves up there.'

Broérec thought for a moment and then began to rock with silent laughter.

'Oh yes, my friend. You are right. We must surrender. But where are Thustan and Drogon?'

'They were at the rear with the dogs.'

'God's wounds! Do you think they were caught by the avalanche?'

'Not a bit of it, Broérec. I think, on the contrary, we shall be seeing them again very soon.'

'What do you mean?'

'Give your orders, Broérec. Your men are waiting, as are the men on the other side.'

Broérec turned to his crouching soldiers.

'Sheathe your swords, men,' he shouted. 'We are giving ourselves up.'

Then he continued in a lower voice.

'Put your daggers up your sleeves and be ready to draw them at my signal.'

The men obeyed.

'We surrender,' shouted Broérec.

A moment passed before the bellowing voice came again.

'Come out of there, one by one. You will not be harmed.'

It was at this moment that Galeran realised to whom the voice belonged. The dark monk, his hood still masking his face, stood just a few feet away from them, escorted by four sturdy fellows armed with heavy maces.

'Do not be afraid,' said Withénoc. 'I give you my word that you will be safe.'

The soldiers came out from behind the rocks and stood waiting for their leader's orders. Broérec passed in front of

153

them and walked slowly towards the monk, his hands raised above his head.

'Throw down your sword,' said Withénoc, eyeing the scimitar that hung by the giant's side.

'It is in its sheath,' protested Broérec. 'What are you afraid of, you coward? Do you think I could draw it faster than one of your men could loose an arrow?'

Galeran, who had followed close behind him, now spoke up.

'So, Withénoc, we meet again. You are more talkative now than you were in Lannédern.'

'Sir Galeran,' replied the monk in his unpleasantly dull voice. 'I did warn you that this is a dangerous land for the curious.'

He suddenly broke off. From above came a long cry of terror. The men looked up and saw a man hurtling down the cliff and come to a thudding halt a few steps away from the false monk. A bloody stump hung at the place where his leg should have been. The silhouette of one of the mastiffs flashed across the clifftop.

The monk and his henchmen looked at each other in stupefaction. Broérec, for his part, now knew that his son had somehow managed to climb up the steep sides of the gorge and move in behind the archers. He saw that this was the moment to attack.

'Draw your swords, men! Kill these pigs!'

He drew his scimitar and ran at Withénoc, brandishing the blade above his head like a metal banner. The monk's men gave a cry and launched at him, swinging their huge maces.

Galeran pulled out his sword and stood by Broérec. He dodged a blow, then lunged forward and plunged his blade into his adversary's groin. Pulling out the bloody point of the sword, he turned and with a terrible cry brought his weapon down on the head of a second man who came at him. He heard the familiar whistle of a scimitar as it rent the air and saw a third man fall at his feet.

The last of Withénoc's four escorts hesitated a moment in the face of this carnage. His hesitation proved fatal, for Broérec chopped off his head with a single slice of his curved sword.

'You have not lost your touch,' exclaimed Galeran. 'Watch out behind you!'

Withénoc was running at Broérec's back with a small dagger in his hand, but Galeran stepped in and nicked his throat with his sword.

'By my faith, move another inch and you are a dead monk!' cried the knight.

Withénoc let his knife slip out of his fingers. Then he turned slowly to face Galeran, drawing back his hood to reveal the impassive face that had so frightened Kaourintin. He stared at the knight, his pupils shrunk as though the light of day was painful to him. Galeran lowered his sword.

'Well, monk,' he said, wondering at the man's strange countenance, 'it appears fate is not looking kindly on you.'

Withénoc, apparently unperturbed by his predicament, said nothing.

'Walk ahead of me,' said Galeran. 'And don't try to escape or I'll skewer you.'

'What do you think I could do, alone and without a weapon?' said the monk with a shrug of his shoulders.

'Keep your distance, Withénoc. I do not know your strength, but I have come to appreciate your deceit.'

He pushed the man forward with the point of his sword, and followed him. Behind him came Broérec and the soldiers, all the while scanning the clifftop for further signs of the enemy. But they saw nothing. Nothing living, at least, for in the stream a few mangled corpses bled steadily into the water.

No more arrows came down at them. But from time to time they heard piercing shrieks followed by furious barking. The archers seemed to have their hands full with Drogon's dogs.

When the men arrived at the foot of the steps that led into the mine they found no one alive. Drogon, Thustan and the dogs had massacred whatever lay in their path, and many of the dead had had their throats slit.

An archer lay in a pool of blood at the foot of the stone steps that led into the mine. Half his jaw had been bitten away by one of the mastiffs, but the man was still alive, for he groaned faintly and his hand twitched. Broérec bent down and slit open his throat.

'He was about to die anyway,' he muttered at Galeran.

The knight spotted Drogon above him on the platform. A man wearing the thick leather apron of a foundry worker was on his knees before him, begging to be spared. By the time the knight and the rest of Broérec's soldiers had climbed up the stairs, the man was already lying dead. Drogon had pierced his heart with his sword.

'Why did you kill him?' asked Broérec. 'He was not even armed.'

'I give no quarter,' hissed Drogon.

His brow was covered in sweat and he was breathing heavily. He was drunk with the sight of blood.

'If Thustan and the dogs had done their work properly they would all be dead by now,' he said.

'You could have left some for us,' said Broérec.

Barks and cries of horror came from one of the underground galleries that opened onto the platform.

'Listen, Broérec, those are children screaming. Here, you take charge of him,' said Galeran, pushing Withénoc towards one of the soldiers. 'Guard him with your life.'

Followed by Drogon and Broérec, he began running towards the source of the screams, and soon arrived at the room that served as the children's dormitory.

Kaourintin and Goranton had managed to keep the grille in place by jamming it with a heavy wooden pole. Thustan and the dogs were hurling themselves at this barricade. The hounds were covered in blood. They gripped the bars of the grille with their huge teeth and growled at the children cowering behind it. Kaourintin and Goranton stood with

156

stones in their hands, ready to use them against the dogs when they broke through.

'Drogon, call off your dogs!' shouted Galeran. 'Thustan, move and you are a dead man. Put down your axe or I'll run you through with my sword.'

'You dare give me orders?' growled Drogon, his jaw set in a terrible rictus.

'Do as he says!' roared Broérec, grabbing his son by the shoulders. 'Call off your dogs. They are only children. It's finished, Drogon.'

A long low whistle came from Drogon's lips. The mastiffs halted their attack and ran to their master, whimpering like pups. Thustan hesitated a moment, then dropped his axe at the knight's feet with a shrug of his shoulders.

'What had you in mind?' asked Galeran. 'Do you want to leave no one alive in the mine?'

'Who are all these children?' asked Broérec, staring in astonishment at the crowd who now pushed against the grille.

'These are the children who disappeared, from Braspartz, from Saint-Herbot and all the other places,' replied Galeran. 'And, as you can see, from Lannédern.'

He went and opened the grille.

'You have saved us, sir,' said Kaourintin. 'Without your intervention, this devil and his dogs would have murdered us.'

The boy was still trembling with fear. Galeran placed a hand on his shoulder.

'It's over now, Kaourintin. Everything will be better now. Take your children outside and wait by the river. Let them rest and warm themselves in the sun, for the journey back will be hard for them.'

'I will do as you say,' said the shepherd, motioning to his little troop to follow him.

The knight felt a little hand taking his and looked down to see a girl, ragged and filthy, staring back up at him.

'May God shield you, sir. I will never forget you.'

'Who are you, girl?'

'I am called Mônik and I am from Braspartz. Tell me your name and I shall pray to the Virgin for you.'

'I am Galeran de Lesneven,' he said, studying the girl's exhausted face. 'You look as if you have been here a long time.'

'Oh yes, sir. A long time. It was like being in Hell without being dead.'

Galeran, moved by the child's words, stroked her cheek. She ran off towards the light, and when she got outside she fell to her knees, dazzled by the day. One of the other children took her gently by the shoulders and led her down to the river.

32

Galeran left the gallery with a sigh of relief. Death and desolation seemed to seep from the walls of this place. Broérec had ordered his men to search the mine from top to bottom, but they found no one. All the guards who had not been killed appeared to have fled. Thustan had disappeared. But Drogon was still with his father's men on the platform.

The soldiers had carried many bodies out to the platform, as well as numerous ingots of lead and silver.

'Even if there were not that many of them, the guards here let themselves be taken rather easily,' thought Galeran. 'The only living witness to the whole affair is Withénoc.'

He turned to the monk, who stood imperturbable, next to the soldier who guarded him.

'Well, Withénoc, you must feel very lonely now.'

The monk did not respond. Galeran saw that he was staring at Drogon, who had his back turned to them as he watched the comings and goings of the soldiers.

'Withénoc,' said Galeran, grabbing the man's arm, 'come with me. We must talk.'

'I can tell you nothing that you do not already know,' said the monk, looking away.

'You are brave in your own way,' said the knight, 'and cunning as a fox. But do you think that is enough to save your life?'

'I will be dead before I can open my mouth, and you know it. In fact, I am already dead, but I do not wish to go alone.'

'There is indeed nothing sadder than going to the gallows without company! Perhaps I can arrange something, Withénoc, but first you must talk with Broérec. Come, down we go. You first.'

He manoeuvred the monk towards the stone steps. Broérec,

who was well satisfied with this expedition as he believed it would not only solve his problems with the peasants but also significantly boost his finances, was talking animatedly with his men. The only shadow in the otherwise favourable situation was Jestin's continuing absence. He had asked Kaourintin and the other children but they had no news of him.

He put the matter out of his mind for the moment, and sent two men off to fetch the horses. He ordered the rest of his soldiers to form a chain to carry the booty out of the mine, and stood watching gleefully as the ingots piled up.

'The monk has something to tell you, Broérec,' said Galeran, pushing Withénoc towards the giant.

'And what might that be?' asked Broérec. 'Were you in charge here?'

'No. The head man here was . . .'

They were the last words ever to leave his lips. There was a whistling sound, then the monk gave a start, turned slowly to one side and fell heavily to the ground. A long arrow with brown fledging was planted just behind his ear, and blood spurted out of the wound. He had died before reaching the ground, his face deformed by a horrible grimace.

Galeran stared for a moment in a stupor, then threw himself on Broérec. The two men rolled to the ground, seeking cover. But no more arrows were fired. Drogon suddenly came running up to his father.

'Father, are you hit?'

'I am fine,' said Broérec, getting to his feet. 'Your dogs must have missed that archer.'

'I have already sent them to correct that mistake. Whoever shot that arrow will not be much longer for this world. He must have been aiming for you but hit that cursed monk instead, so there is no great loss.'

'On the contrary,' retorted Galeran, 'the loss is immense. Withénoc was the last witness who could have shed some light on this strange affair.'

'Why should we need witnesses, knight?' asked Drogon

sarcastically. 'We have captured a fortune here, and now the children can go back to their villages. All is for the best!'

'Drogon is right,' agreed Broérec, patting his son on the back. 'Why should we care for the life of this bastard who would anyhow have ended up hanging from a rope? Or we might have handed him over to the villagers to let them have some sport.'

Galeran turned away, profoundly dissatisfied. But his face lit up when he saw a slender figure advancing along the gorge.

'Look, Broérec,' he said. 'I told you you would see him again, and there he is.'

Broérec looked and saw his young son walking nimbly towards him. Next to him was Hoël, pushing along in front of him a limping, bloodied Thustan.

Galeran glanced at Drogon. The young man's face had turned a sickly grey, and he had moved back a step.

Jestin strode up to his father and threw down at his feet a quiver full of arrows with brown fledging.

'Look, Father, these are of the same type as the arrow that killed the monk. The next one would have been for you if Hoël had not overpowered this murderer,' he said, pointing an accusing finger at Thustan.

'What is this?' bellowed Broérec. 'Say something, Thustan. Defend yourself!'

But Thustan merely stood there, shaking his head.

'Right, Jestin,' exploded Broérec, 'tell me exactly what is going on here. You disappear for days on end and then when you do come back you are allied with this bastard!'

Hoël paled, and was about to reply when Jestin took him by the arm.

'No, Hoël, let my father speak.'

'Tell me, what are you doing in his company?' insisted Broérec, alarmed by the understanding between his favourite son and this hated enemy.

'Father,' Jestin replied calmly, 'you would do better to put

161

these questions to Drogon. He alone will be able to answer them.'

'What are you saying, you runt!' roared Drogon.

'As my brother does not wish to reply, I shall do so in his place,' continued Jestin. 'Thustan killed the monk because he wanted to silence him for ever. If you cannot guess why, then Drogon will be able to tell you.'

'I'll stick that in your throat!' cried Drogon, launching at Jestin with his dagger and stabbing his side.

Jestin jumped back and pulled out his sword. He stood, blood flowing from his wound, and made ready to fight.

'That's enough, you two!' shouted Broérec, who feared he was losing control of the situation.

'This is between Drogon and me, Father,' said Jestin. 'Please keep out of it.'

Broérec hesitated, and Galeran now intervened.

'Drogon, you would have to kill not only Jestin, but both Hoël and myself to keep your secrets safe. Your game is lost.'

'Then I may as well finish it without further ado,' Drogon said savagely.

He drew his sword and with it struck Jestin's weapon with such force that it flew out of his hand and landed several feet away. Jestin was shaken, but stood his ground, ready to fight to the end. He pulled out the dagger that hung from his belt.

'Do not move, Hoël,' he said in a voice noticeably higher than before. 'Father, Drogon is behind all of this. He wanted you dead.'

He moved back slowly until his body was almost against the cliff.

'Why should he believe you?' cried Drogon, rushing at him with his sword. 'Prepare to die, Jestin. We shall meet in Hell!'

Jestin stumbled and fell back. He tried to thrust with his dagger, but it was too late. Drogon was already upon him. He closed his eyes as a spurt of blood washed over his face.

*

When he reopened them the first thing he saw was Drogon's headless corpse lying on the pebbly ground next to him. Broérec stood beside his dead son, wiping the blood from his scimitar.

Jestin fell into a faint. Galeran and Hoël were at his side when he came to. Broérec sat a little distance away at the bank of the stream, muttering to himself. The soldiers stood in a circle around the decapitated body. A strange silence hung over the place, broken only by Broérec's mumbling. The children waited a little distance away, unnerved by the violence.

'How are you feeling, girl?' asked the knight, examining the cut on Jestin's side. 'You will soon be better, for your wound is but a slight one.'

'Say something, Ninian,' said Hoël, squeezing her hand.

But Ninian just stared at them without a word.

'Do not fear, Hoël,' said Galeran. 'She will be fine, she is still in shock. Please see to her wound while I speak with Broérec.'

He felt a great weariness as he walked slowly over to the giant. He called to the men-at-arms, who stood stupefied by the carnage.

'Don't stand there gaping! Make up some stretchers to carry the wounded. We'll see to the ingots later.'

The soldiers shook off their lethargy and got to work. Galeran heard a familiar whinny and saw two soldiers arriving with Quolibet and the other horses.

Galeran went over to Broérec and laid a compassionate hand on his shoulder. The giant, who hardly seemed to notice his presence, went on muttering incomprehensibly.

'He is dead, Broérec,' said the knight. 'He would have killed Jestin. You know that.'

Broérec raised his pitiful face to him.

'I killed him, Galeran, I killed my own son! All is black for me now. The only reality is evil, the Devil, pain. Nothing else exists! There is too much hatred, too much blood . . .'

'It is between you and your conscience now. But I would have done it if you had not.'

'That I know. But there are so many things here I do not understand. Do you really think Drogon was behind it all?'

'Let us speak of that later. First let us return to the château.'

'What about the bastard? What is he doing with Jestin?'

'That is another story, Broérec,' said the knight with a smile. 'But at this moment when you have lost a son, perhaps you should think again about the rest of your offspring.'

'What do you mean?'

'You are intelligent enough to understand without my having to explain.'

Broérec lowered his eyes. Then he stood up and turned to Galeran.

'You are right. Let us go back. I need to think. He can come with us if he wants,' he added, nodding in the direction of Hoël, who was dressing Jestin's wound.

The soldiers had just finished burying the dead near the cairns when Broérec gave the signal to depart. Galeran had, with Kaourintin's help, tended the wounded. They removed arrows and cauterised the wounds with a knife they had heated over a flame.

The journey back to the château was long and silent. The Lord of Huelgoat led the way, his son's bloody body draped across the back of his saddle. Galeran followed behind, carrying Mônik on his shoulders and leading Quolibet by the reins. Three children were perched on the horse's broad back. The soldiers had also let some of the children ride their horses. The stronger ones walked behind Kaourintin and Goranton, and the sick were laid on stretchers carried by the men-at-arms. At the rear came Jestin and Hoël and their prisoner.

A savage cry sounded in the distance. It was impossible to

say whether it came from a dog or a wolf. Drogon's hounds had not been seen since their assault on the clifftop archers.

Galeran wondered whether they were still pursuing some unfortunate across the forest or whether, maddened by blood and the death of their master, they had returned to the wild. He imagined them running free, hunting for pleasure in the dark hills of Arez, and he saw them plunging into the green and foaming waters of the Youdik, ferrymen for Drogon's damned soul.

PART FIVE

Qui sert, n'est pas libre;
Qui sent, n'est pas mort;
Qui désire, veut;
Qui veut, mendie . . .

He who serves, is not free;
He who feels, is not dead;
He who desires, must have;
He who must have, shall beg . . .

Marguerite Porète

33

When they arrived at the château they found a little group of peasants waiting for them. They had been led there by Gweltaz and now sat in a circle near the entrance. The old priest from Lannédern was also there, as was young Armelle. Titik had carried Galeran's message to Gweltaz telling him to come with the priest, and together they had rounded up the village's strongest men.

The lookouts in the château gave the alarm when they saw the band approaching, but Gweltaz had called out to them and persuaded them to let the group wait by the drawbridge for Broérec's return.

'Good day to you, Père Gwen,' Galeran called as he gently lowered Mônik to the ground. 'And to you, Gweltaz. Thank you for coming so quickly.'

'Good day to you, knight,' said the priest, staring in wonder at the group of children who stood around Kaourintin. 'I came to bury Dame Génovéfa and her boy. I see God has helped you in your quest, and that He has also answered my prayers.'

'I greet you, Galeran de Lesneven,' said Gweltaz. 'May God shield you.'

He looked at the corpse that hung over Broérec's horse, at the wounded on the stretchers, and at the chains that held Thustan.

'I see that my men will be of little use to you. You seem to have come through this trial without our help.'

'Praise be to God,' replied Galeran.

Two boys broke away from the group of children and ran to Gweltaz.

'It's us, it's us!' they cried.

The old man looked at them a moment before recognising their thin and hungry faces as those of Janik's sons.

'Well, well, boys! You're in a fine state. Your mother will never recognise you.'

'Yes, but at least we're still alive!' replied the elder of the pair.

'You are absolutely right!' said the old man joyously. 'And you'll soon get back to your robust old selves, we shall see to that.'

Then he turned to Broérec and addressed him for the first time in a long while.

'Sir Broérec, may I accompany them back to the village?'

'You may,' growled Broérec. 'But what the devil is this crowd doing here in front of my château? And who is that girl?'

'I asked them to come, Broérec,' Galeran interrupted. 'These men might have been very useful to us if luck had not been on our side.'

'Very well. Let these three come inside with us,' said Broérec, gesturing towards the priest, Gweltaz and Armelle. 'It is fortunate that you are here, for I am in need of a priest.'

'I am at your service,' said Père Gwen.

'But the rest will stay outside,' Broérec added haughtily. 'I will have no peasants in my château.'

The drawbridge was lowered and the little troop entered the courtyard. Broérec dismounted and took his son's body down from the saddle. He pushed his way through the crowd of soldiers and carried his burden towards the keep. Galeran saw Cléophas come out to meet him. The old man stood to one side to let his master pass, and then the pair of them disappeared inside.

The knight helped the three children climb down from Quolibet and gave them over to Anna who, with Armelle's help, was taking charge of the situation.

'Well, Armelle,' said Galeran mischievously, 'what brings you here? I don't recall sending for you.'

The girl blushed.

'I thought you might need me,' she mumbled.

'I myself have no need of you. But there is a certain shepherd by the name of Kaourintin who might like to see you. Go to him, my dear Armelle. In the space of one day he has lost much and gained much. I think you will find him greatly changed.'

The girl did not need to be told twice. Galeran watched her run off, and saw Kaourintin moving away from the group of children to come to meet her. Hand in hand, the pair went to sit by the cistern to tell each other their tales.

'Sir Galeran, my lord has sent me to ask you what you wish us to do with all these people.' A man-at-arms, a sergeant who took charge of the château whenever Broérec was absent, stood deferentially before him.

'First give them something to eat and find some warm clothes for those that lack them. Put the wounded in the kitchen and have Thustan brought to the upper room. See to it that he is chained; he will be your responsibility.'

'Yes, sir,' said the sergeant, turning on his heels.

Galeran led Quolibet to the stable and returned to the courtyard to find Père Gwen in discussion with Gweltaz.

'Come, Gweltaz,' he called out. 'We must bring this affair to a close. Père Gwen and Kaourintin, please join us in the upper room. I shall fetch Broérec.'

'Very well, sir. And these two?' asked Gweltaz, motioning towards Hoël and Ninian, who stood together in the middle of the courtyard.

'Let them come as well,' replied the knight, walking off towards the keep.

34

They all sat in the upper room of the keep. Broérec was slumped over the table, Hoël and Jestin huddled next to each other on a bench, Père Gwen and Gweltaz sat uneasily beside them, and young Kaourintin stood behind them. Cléophas squatted on a low stool, and at his feet sat Titik.

The three candles of death burned in the room, a reminder that Drogon's body reposed in the box bed.

The gathering was like a family reunion, but this was a family ravaged by hatred and bloodshed. All eyes were fixed on Galeran.

'It is time,' the knight said slowly, 'to try to make some sense of this business, which for most of us has been and still is like an abominable dream.'

Broérec interrupted him.

'Galeran, I called you here because ever since my return from captivity I have been living in this monstrous dream of which you speak – to such a degree that I no longer knew whether I was sleeping or waking. I wanted you to deliver me from the nightmare, but it seems you have pushed me even further into it.'

'Broérec,' the knight said softly, 'it is not I who can deliver you, but the truth. Are you ready to hear the truth?'

The giant nodded, but said nothing.

'Certain clergymen and theologians deny original sin,' Galeran began. 'It is unjust, they say, that the transgression of the first man, the father of us all, should wash down over all humanity, that the newborn babe should be tainted by a curse that goes so far back.

'The idea is an appalling one, I admit, but it is one rooted in reality. In truth, our actions and our deeds have a power we can never understand. We die, but the evil we do goes on without us, after us, in one way or another. Thus, Broérec, when greed drove you to keep secret what your father told you on his deathbed, you created your own nightmare, your own Youdik!

'Not only was it a despicable act, but it was also a stupid one. You need not be reminded that times are changing. The great lords are forging alliances to which people like you must submit or be destroyed. A garrison of twenty or thirty men is nothing these days. We have seen from the Crusades that thousands of men are now needed to make war.

'Imagine what would have happened had you properly exploited the mine. Prosperity would have flowed into your land and you would have become more powerful. But this, of course, did not even occur to you. You wanted to satisfy your taste for violence, and embarked on a hazardous military adventure in which you lost not only many years of your young life but also . . . But let us leave that for the moment.'

Broérec, his face ashen grey, fidgeted uneasily as Galeran spoke.

'No,' he growled, 'go on! I want to hear.'

'In this story you gave me the role of intruder. Everywhere I came up against the law of silence. Jestin, Cléophas, Drogon, you yourself, the peasants, Père Gwen . . . Everyone either said nothing or lied. But someone finally made a move. This person went through my belongings and stole the letter you sent me. That was a grave mistake. Why not just read it and put it back in its place? The answer was easy. Whoever stole it was unlettered and took it away to have it read by someone else. So, who could not read and had access to my affairs at that time?

'Drogon, who after the hunt went straight to the keep with his father. Drogon, who had always preferred the hunt to the scriptorium. When Broérec went to his bed, Drogon simply walked to my room and seized the letter. But to whom could he turn to have it deciphered? The answer was not long in coming to me – Dame Génovéfa.'

Cléophas, hearing his wife's name, sat up and looked at the knight with despair in his eyes.

'Yes, my dear Cléophas,' Galeran went on, 'your wife's role was a mystery to me. That Drogon sought to supplant his father, that was understandable. That Thustan was a willing accomplice I could also accept. That Jestin went missing, well, why not? But Dame Génovéfa troubled me. A woman still in her prime, beautiful, educated and rich. What could she be doing here in the far reaches of Armorica? Why had she not packed her bags and left long ago?

'Broérec had forced her to come to his château and married her off against her will to a man who was already old. But in the château dwelt the Valkyrie whom Broérec had wed without her consent. The complicity between the two women was immediate, for they had a common enemy. And that enemy was you, Broérec.'

The giant grew ever paler. He shot Galeran a furious look, made as if to stand up, then slumped back down again.

'Génovéfa quickly gains her mistress's confidence. She hears of the abandoned mine and learns that Mechtilde is in love with a cousin by the name of Siegfried. So she encourages her mistress to write to her lover, who comes running as soon as he gets the letter. Broérec is at war, and Génovéfa's farm serves as the lovers' trysting place. The Lord of Huelgoat has been trying for years to get his wife with child, but in vain. Yet she quickly falls pregnant by Siegfried, who vows to return with a troop of well-armed men and take her away. When he returns Mechtilde is in labour. As soon as she has given birth he carries his beloved away, leaving the child, little Ninian, with Génovéfa and Cléophas, to whom I owe this story.'

Galeran had observed Broérec as he spoke, and expected him to explode at any moment. But the giant now spoke in a voice that was eerily calm.

'Go on, Galeran, go on. I must know everything.'

'When they had crossed the Rhine Dame Mechtilde became

a bigamist by marrying the man she loved. But the Church, as you know, forbids marriage between cousins, and excommunicated the couple. They then left for the Holy Land, where they met their deaths.'

Hoël wheeled round to face Ninian.

'But that's the story you told me!'

'I swear to you I did not know,' replied the girl. 'Pére Gwen told it to me but he never said who it was about.'

'The tragic history of your parents has become famous throughout the Christian world, my dear girl,' said Galeran. 'You would have to be a heathen like Broérec not to have heard it. But that was only the first act of the mystery that was played out here.'

The knight now looked at Broérec.

'I always considered you a brute but I never underestimated the keenness of your spirit. You were driven mad by the jealousy Mechtilde inspired in you, and your jealousy was justified. You chased all women from your household, and here again you were right, at least as far as Dame Génovéfa was concerned!

'When Cléophas finally deigned to speak to me it was to advise me to go and see his wife. Which I did the very next day. Génovéfa was not pleased, but she hid this very well, for she was a fine actress. She fed me small pieces of information in the way a hunter might leave bait for his prey.

'But the facts spoke for themselves. She did not belong there on the farm in that forsaken place. Unless . . . But let us now turn to her tragic death, shall we not, Thustan?'

Thustan stared defiantly at the knight, his chains rattling gently.

'You were not there when I returned to the château that day. In fact, you had followed me to the farm. You waited there after I left, and chance came to your aid. Dame Génovéfa, her son and the old servant went out to the orchard . . .'

Old Cléophas leapt to his feet.

'So it was you, villain!' he cried.

Thustan said nothing, but suddenly there was terror in his rolling eyes. The beast within him had departed, leaving only a human wreck.

'Come, calm yourself,' Galeran told Cléophas. 'There could only have been one reason why Dame Génovéfa did not leave the farm, and that reason was the mine. For the mine could bring her both power and money. She was, thanks to Dame Mechtilde, one of the few people who knew of its existence. So she craftily took charge of Drogon as he grew into a young man. She became his mistress, turned him against his father and filled his head with plans for secretly reopening the mine. This was not difficult, for, Broérec, you took to drink after your wife ran off, and no longer harboured any military ambitions.

'Dame Génovéfa was not satisfied with her dowry. She wanted more, very much more. No doubt she also dreamed of one day marrying this son of a lord whom she knew she could dominate. The only problem with the mine was finding workers. Skilled miners demanded high wages. And the galleries were very small. This is where Withénoc stepped in.

'Cléophas told me Drogon liked to visit the bawdy houses in Carhaix; it was no doubt there that he met the monk. It was also in Carhaix that a young shepherd boy was calling for a children's Crusade without knowing that he would be leading his flock to Hell. Am I right, Kaourintin?'

'Yes, it is true,' mumbled the boy. 'Withénoc came to see me in the marketplace, and I could not refuse his offer of help . . .'

'You served as bait to catch a very unusual sort of prey, Kaourintin. Dame Génovéfa was like a slave trader who sends children to the Orient. Thanks to you she found the workforce she needed. She was on the best of terms with her neighbours, for she paid them handsomely. In exchange, they shut their eyes to what was going on, although they were unaware of the truly monstrous scale of the woman's doings.

'Ah, yes! She thought of everything, did Dame Génovéfa. Everything except Thustan. They say that wolves will never eat each other, so we must conclude that they are less cruel than men. One day this brute here had enough of being a mere flunkey. Silver was flowing past him and he got only a paltry sum for his efforts. He knew that Broérec would not be around for very much longer. His death had been delayed a little by my arrival. But if he were to learn Dame Génovéfa's secrets he would know as much as Drogon and would be able to take control.

'But Thustan is a stupid fool,' continued the knight. 'He succeeded in buying off Génovéfa's servants, but could get nothing out of the lady herself after he had killed her son. From then on, Drogon was watching him and, as we have seen, he had to hurry.'

'But why,' asked the old priest in a quavering voice, 'did Withénoc come to Lannédern?'

'Your village, deep within the hills of Arez, served as a refuge. All these children would have aroused too much suspicion in a town. And the man knew he could intimidate you.'

'Why did he not deliver us directly to the mine?' asked Kaourintin.

'Withénoc was cunning. He knew that if you stayed there other children would come to join you. And he wanted to fatten you up a little before selling you.'

'Then why did he deliver Janik's boys before us?' Kaourintin insisted.

'Even if he had realised that he would lose some children along the way, he had not planned for all the bodies which would have to be got rid of. So he delivered new slaves to replace any that died.'

'If it was not the people in the mine who were killing the children, who was it then?' asked Broérec.

'You may recall, Broérec, that I spoke to you of poison, and not of a poisoner. There is, of course, a considerable difference. I promised you I would find the culprit and I have kept my word. Here it is.'

He reached into his pouch and pulled out an object which he threw down on the table. Everyone in the room looked at the thing and saw that it was a bluish-grey ingot.

'What is this?' cried Broérec.

'The children were killed by cold metal. And I think your father met his end the same way. The poisoner was the lead that they scratched with their nails and whose fine and deadly dust they breathed in day and night.'

'How did you come to realise this?'

'It was the blue-black line on their gums that showed me what sort of poison it was. When I saw the state of the dead children's knees, it was merely a question of finding a mine that had galleries so small that even a child had to crawl to pass through them.'

The knight's words were met with a stupefied silence. He now walked over to Broérec, who sat staring in dejection at the floor.

'You rejected the son whose soul was noble and who, in the end, saved your life. But you are still his father, whether you wish it or not. You humiliated Cléophas, who was a loyal ally. Without these two, and without, of course, little Titik, we would not be here now.'

35

Kaourintin sighed deeply as he left the keep. The cool air was very welcome after the oppressive atmosphere of the upper room. A little figure emerged from the shadow of the draw-bridge and ran to him.

'Kaourintin?' said an anxious voice.

The boy gave a start.

'Armelle! What are you doing here?'

She looked at him, and, as always when she was with him, did not know whether to laugh or cry.

'I just wanted to see if you were well.'

'I am as well as anyone can be who has a troubled conscience.'

'You must not blame yourself, Kaourintin! You always acted in good faith.'

'My good faith has cost so many children their lives!' he said bitterly. 'Innocents died because of me. My life will not be long enough to make amends.' He sighed again.

'But please forgive me, Armelle. I am speaking of myself again. It is nearly dark. You must get home, for your mother will be worried.'

'Gweltaz promised he would tell her I am safe. He has just left with his men and said I could wait here for you. I shall go back with Père Gwen when he comes out.'

'Broérec asked him to hear his confession, so I suspect he will be some time.' The shepherd boy could not help but smile as he said this. Armelle laughed.

'I wonder if he will really tell him everything!' she said. 'He could be there for days on end. But do tell me what happened up there, Kaourintin. They all looked very strange when they came out.'

'I'll tell you everything when we get back to Lannédern. As the priest cannot accompany you, please let me.'

It was with some relief that the pair left the château and walked into the forest. Birds called in the treetops, and the air was fresh and calm. It was dusk, and the stars were beginning to shine in the blue depth of the sky.

Armelle said nothing during the long walk. But Kaourintin talked and talked and talked, as though he had all the sins of the world to confess. He told his companion that he would take all the children back to their homes, even if it took him a year to do so. He finished by saying he would not return to Daoulas.

Suddenly Armelle stopped and turned to face him. Her grey eyes held his as she spoke.

'"He shall show me the Holy City, he shall show me Jerusalem descending from Heaven . . ." I shall await your return, Kaourintin! Then we shall leave for the new world, and this time it will be for real.'

When they arrived at Lannédern they were walking side by side, their fingers entwined.

36

Night had long fallen by the time Broérec left the little room where Père Gwen had heard his confession. The old priest climbed slowly and wearily down the steps to the kitchen. The ardour of Broérec's repentance had exhausted him. Gweltaz had ordered some men to stay behind and accompany him back to Lannédern, and at the same time to bring with them the bodies of Génovéfa and her son and servant. The little band left the château and was soon swallowed up in the darkness.

Galeran saw fierce resolution in Broérec's face. But he also noted that for the first time since he had known him, the giant seemed at peace with himself. Had he perhaps received posthumous pardon for the sins of his father at the same time as forgiveness for his own misdeeds?

The knight, who had decided to leave the next morning for Léon, placed a hand on the giant's shoulder.

'May I speak with you a moment, Broérec?'

'Yes, my friend.'

'My task here is finished. My debt is paid, and now I shall return to my home.'

'You have done much more than pay your debt, Galeran. I am now in debt to you.'

'No, Broérec, I absolve you. If you find peace and contentment then I shall have been doubly repaid.'

'When do you leave?'

'Tomorrow at dawn.'

'May I ask another favour of my comrade-in-arms?'

Galeran considered the man's calm face and wondered whether some inner fury might still be hidden beneath it.

'Ask,' he said.

'I have sworn before Père Gwen and before God to atone

for my sins. Tomorrow at first light I shall do penance before my men and before the peasants, whom Gweltaz has promised to summon.'

'You wish your penance to be public?' asked Galeran incredulously.

'Yes, I do. I ask for your assistance only until the moment when the drawbridge is lowered tomorrow morning. I would like you to help me through this night.'

Galeran agreed.

'There is one last thing I wanted to ask of you,' said Broérec. 'It is something very dear to me. I have thought about what you said regarding Hoël. I think that once he has spent some time in the service of a lord, he should wear the white cloak of a knight, for his lineage gives him the right to do so.'

Galeran nodded approvingly.

'I shall send him to Vicomte Tanguy. When he is due to become a knight I should like you to attend the ceremony, for there could be no better mentor for him. And at this ceremony I would like you to give him my sword.'

'Why will not you do this yourself?'

'I have decided that when my penance is done and I have put my affairs in order, I shall set out for Landévennec.'

'To join the Abbey of Saint-Guénolé?'

'Yes. Père Gwen is a friend of the abbot, and is planning to go and see him in the spring. I shall go with him. It appears that the Benedictines need strong men to help them build a fortified castle beside the sea.'

Broérec's eyes sparkled mischievously.

'I'll wager you never expected to see this happen, Galeran. Broérec de Huelgoat a monk! For once I surprise you. If I do not make a good monk, then perhaps I could run the abbey's storehouse and wine cellar. I hear they have excellent vineyards there.'

Then he spoke more seriously.

'Do you think they will have me?'

'I should feel sorry for them if they do,' said Galeran with a smile.

'But I am capable of gentleness,' protested Broérec, joining his hands as though for prayer.

The knight looked at him and burst out laughing. Broérec's fist swung at him and he managed to jump aside just in time.

'I think you need to work on your gentleness,' laughed Galeran.

The giant, shocked at himself, stared in disbelief at his huge hands.

'You are right, Galeran; but I know I can do it.'

'I believe you, for I know you are as stubborn as a mule.'

They stood a while without a word, each considering his own future.

'You have not answered the question I put to you earlier,' said Broérec, breaking the silence. 'Will you be Hoël's mentor and attend his dubbing?'

'I will. Hoël is a fine young man. He will make a valiant knight.'

'I hope what you say is true,' murmured Broérec.

'What about Jestin? Or Ninian, I mean.'

'I shall return to bless her union with my son. I hope you will come too.'

'I thought I was ridding myself of you, Broérec,' said the knight with a laugh. 'Now here you are binding me ever closer to you!'

'I now understand why, when we were in Vitré, I always preferred your company to that of the others. There are few as valiant as you, Galeran. So it is in my interest to link you to my family for good.'

With these words he gave the knight a resounding thump on the back.

37

The night was long. Broérec had talked until the dawn came to announce a new day. Galeran was tired, but he felt joy at the thought of returning to his home in Léon. From below he heard the clatter of plates and someone humming gaily to himself. He climbed swiftly down the long ladder to the kitchen. The voice he had heard belonged to Cléophas, and this surprised him as the old man had been so sombre the previous evening, and had even had to be helped out of the room by Titik.

Cléophas was emptying water from a pot when the knight arrived. He turned to him and smiled warmly.

'Good day, Cléophas! You seem very happy today.'

'Good day, sir,' came the somewhat embarrassed reply. 'You must be hungry. I'll make you something nice.'

He took a plump sausage from the salting tub and began grilling it over the fire. He stood with his back to the knight, his attention now focused on his task.

Suddenly a groaning noise came from the cellar. Galeran looked and saw a ladder protruding from the trapdoor. He recalled that he had ordered a soldier to guard the entrance. There was no sign of the man now.

'What is going on down there? Has the guard gone down to see Thustan?'

'Er, no,' muttered Cléophas, growing ever more ill at ease. 'The guard has gone out.'

'And left the ladder there? What are you hiding from me, Cléophas?'

He went to the trapdoor and climbed down the ladder. There was silence when he got to the bottom. He stopped for a moment to let his eyes adapt to the semi-darkness. By the smoky light of a torch the first thing he saw was Thustan's chained body doubled over by the millstone. The knight knew already what he was about to find. He walked over to the dead man. Foam dribbled from the side of a mouth that was twisted in pain. A bowl lay at his feet. Galeran picked it up and sniffed the pungent odour that rose up from it.

There was no other poison as powerful as this. The ancients knew it. Henbane, for that is what it was, grew like weeds in ruins. Its effect was swift, and the pain it caused before finally bringing on death was unbearable.

There was nothing Galeran could do for the man, for his soul had left his body. He climbed back up the ladder, bearing the bowl in his hand. He found Cléophas waiting for him, shifting from one foot to the other. Galeran looked at him severely.

'Cléophas, I have always said your food was inedible. And now Thustan has died from indigestion!'

38

The drawbridge was lowered and a murmur ran through the throng on the parade ground in front of the château. There were people from Huelgoat, Saint-Herbot and Lannédern, and from many other villages and outlying farms. Gweltaz Ar Fur had done his duty and sent out messengers to announce the public penance of the Lord of Huelgoat. It was such a singular event, and the crimes of Broérec and his son were so many and so great, that few wished to miss the spectacle.

There was silence in the courtyard of the château. Galeran had ordered the men-at-arms to form two long lines that stretched from the foot of the keep to the drawbridge. They stood like statues in their coats of mail, their weapons by their side, to pay final homage to their lord.

Hoël and Ninian stood a little to one side, awed by this ceremony that seemed more military than religious. Old Cléophas, his hands resting on Titik's frail shoulders, observed the scene from the door of his kitchen.

Broérec emerged from the keep and drew himself up to his full height. He looked more than ever like a Dane. He was dressed only in dark breeches, his chest was bare, and his long blond hair fell down over his shoulders. A long whip hung from his left hand.

Galeran stood a little behind him. Broérec turned to him, his face even paler than usual after his sleepless night.

'Come what may, we shall meet again, my brother-in-arms. I know it.'

'May God give you strength,' replied the knight.

Galeran watched the giant walk, his head held high, past the lines of soldiers. He began to flagellate himself as he neared the drawbridge. The silence that reigned in the courtyard amplified the crack of the whip. Long weals appeared on his shoulders and back. The Lord of Huelgoat grimaced but made no sound.

Père Gwen, who stood just outside the château, made the sign of the cross, shocked by Broérec's controlled violence. The peasants moved aside to let their lord pass. They had not expected such ferocity. Many of them followed Gweltaz's example and turned and headed for home.

In his way, Broérec had won again. He remained the master, a man who controlled suffering and death, including his own. Galeran knew he would carry on as far as Lannédern and would then return to the château that evening to collapse at the foot of the keep, his body bathed in blood and his penance complete. Like those Crusaders who had the cross of Christ sewn onto their right shoulder, Broérec had chosen to write his punishment on his flesh. In this manner the Lord of Huelgoat paid for the soul of the father whose soul he had allowed to be damned, for the mothers of Hoël and Drogon, for Dame Mechtilde, for his son, for all those he had pitilessly punished, raped and killed.

The knight turned away. The long night and the horror of the past days combined to make him feel nauseous. He took a deep breath and told himself that now, finally, it was time to go home. He thought dreamily of the little chapel on the beach and the infinite expanse of the ocean.

Broérec's silhouette disappeared round a bend in the path, closely followed by a large group of praying peasants.

39

Galeran leaned back against the wall of the ruined chapel and watched the sun sink into the sea. The beach was covered in a thick snow-white carpet: thousands of gulls sat there, motionless, looking out at the ocean. It was a sign that the summer was at an end. The knight watched the birds suddenly fly up to escape the two figures on horseback who galloped along the beach through the breaking waves. One of the horses was white, the other black. As they drew closer he could hear voices rising above the roar of the sea. The voices grew ever clearer, and formed themselves into a song:

> *L'âge qui convient à la guerre . . .*
> *Convient aux soldats de Vénus . . .*
> *. . . l'ardeur d'un vaillant soldat,*
> *La femme la réclame à son amant . . .*

Galeran felt his heartbeat quicken. His eyes were fixed in disbelief on the white steed and the figure dressed in purple and white who sat proudly upon its back. He had regained his composure by the time the pair drew up in front of him, and spoke in a bantering tone as he took the reins of the white stallion.

'My sweet, that is a fine song for a nun to be singing! I thought you were cloistered.'

'And I had no clue where you were, dear knight!' said the woman as she gracefully dismounted.

They walked a few paces together before she turned to him with a smile.

'There is no kingdom in this world that is eternal. Only the kingdom of Our Lord and the kingdom of love.'

'I see your time in the convent has turned you into a philosopher.'

'I was enlightened!'

'Indeed!'

'I soon saw that I was a little too young for the kingdom of God. And a woman's beauty fades quickly if it is not appreciated.'

'That I know well, my dear friend. But you need not fear on that count.'

She laughed and turned to the young equerry who held the horses.

'Diamant,' she called softly, 'take the horses. Come and fetch me tomorrow morning when there remains but one star in the sky.'

The boy bowed, jumped into his saddle and rode away.

The woman loosened her hair and let her long purple robe slide from her body and onto the warm sand of the dunes. Galeran trembled as though it were the first time.

'You know,' he said, taking her in his arms, 'I have often dreamed of you.'

'Then I shall have to inspire you to dream some more . . .'

Que ceci soit la fin du livre mais non la fin de la recherche

Bernard de Clairvaux

189

Author's Note

In his book *Magie de la Bretagne* Anatole le Braz writes of 'the fierce heart of the Arez that lies between Huelgoat and Landernau'.

The road that crosses it, built over an ancient Roman way, goes over hill after hill until it arrives at the sublime Roc'h Trevezel. Here you are on the balcony of the Occident . . . In winter, when the wind is raging, the spectacle is almost Dantesque . . . In summer, at sunset, it becomes magical.

Today, around Huelgoat, one can still see the hills, the gorge, the rocks and the magical lake. Traces can be seen of the mine, which was exploited first by the Celts and then by the Romans, and which was finally shut down for good in 1934. The abbey of Landévennec, where Broérec took refuge, confronted Viking raids, the Hundred Years War and revolution, and has once again become the home of a Benedictine community. Eight hundred years later, its magnificent Romanesque ruins still proudly face the sea and the winds of Finistère.

La Cuisine d'Hermine
Medieval Recipes

Potage de Courges Frangiées de Safran

For 6 people
2kg marrows
150g smoked bacon cubes
½ teaspoon ginger
saffron
salt and pepper

This simple dish takes ten minutes to prepare and around thirty minutes to cook.

Wash, peel and seed the marrows. Cut the skin into julienne strips and dice the flesh.

Brown the bacon in a pan without using oil, add the diced marrow, pour in a little water and cook over a low heat until you have a purée.

Add the spices and season.

Sprinkle the strips of marrow skin and the saffron over the purée. This is what French cooks term *frangier*.

Eau Bénite

This sauce, which our modern palates may find unusual, accompanies roast or boiled meats. It was Hermine's favourite sauce.

½ glass rosewater
1 teaspoon ginger
1 tablespoon marjoram
½ glass verjuice (the acid juice of unripe grapes, apples or
    crab apples)

If you cannot find any verjuice, a strong mustard will suffice
to make a twentieth-century version of *eau bénite*. In this case,
use only three tablespoons of mustard.

Add the ginger and the marjoram to the rosewater and boil
for fifteen minutes.

Add the verjuice or the mustard.

Sieve and pour over the meat.

Tourifas

Hermine serves this dish mostly in winter. It is easily and
quickly made and is handy for using up ham leftovers and
stale bread.

250g diced bacon
1 handful of lean ham, diced
200g mushrooms
chopped parsley and chives
pepper, ginger, cumin, nutmeg, cinnamon
1 lemon
1 egg
slices of bread
flour

Cook the bacon cubes in a little water. Drain.

Put some bacon fat or butter in a pan and sweat the ham
over a low heat. Add the mushrooms, bacon, parsley, chives,
a pinch of flour and a little water. Season with the pepper
and the other spices. Simmer until the mixture thickens and

remove from the heat. Squeeze the lemon over the pan and leave to cool.

Beat the eggs. Dip the bread in the eggs then cover them with the mixture. Cover with breadcrumbs and fry.

Serve piping hot with a full-bodied red wine.

Benoiles

For 6 people
125g flour
4 eggs
50g butter
salt
25g preserved lemon rind
brown sugar
orange blossom water

Pour 25cl water into a pan. Add the butter, cut into small squares. When the butter has melted add a pinch of salt and the lemon rind, cut into fine strips.

Bring to the boil and remove from the heat. Add the flour and stir vigorously with a wooden spoon until you get a smooth batter.

Place over a low heat, stirring continually until all the water has evaporated. Remove from the heat and add one egg to the mixture. Stir briskly.

Repeat this process for the other three eggs. If all the water has evaporated, the batter will quickly absorb the eggs.

In a different pan heat a good depth of oil (or use a deep fryer) until the oil is hot but not boiling.

Take a spoonful of the batter and drop it into the pan. If the oil is at the right temperature the fritter will sink to the bottom and immediately rise again to the top. Continue making fritters in this way, letting them fry for four minutes, then turning them and frying them for another four minutes.

Remove with a skimmer and drain on absorbent paper. Sprinkle with sugar and orange blossom water.

Serve very hot.

Bon appétit!

A Medieval Lexicon

Ankou: a death spirit (literally 'worker of death') in Brittany (*oberour ar maro*)

Ar Fur: Breton for a wise man

Ar Menez Reûn Dû: Breton for the Black Mountain

Ar Moigne: Breton for a one-armed man

Armorica: an ancient name for Brittany

breeches: a garment covering the loins and thighs

Cluny: a town in eastern central France. The reformed Benedictine order was founded there in 910, and it was an important religious and cultural centre throughout the Middle Ages.

dubbing: the ceremony in which a man is made a knight by the ritual of tapping on his shoulder with a sword.

Huelgoat: the 'upper wood', a town in Finistère at the foot of the hills of Arez

Hypocaust: an ancient Roman heating system in which hot air circulated under the floor and between double walls.

league: a unit of distance of varying length, most commonly equal to three miles

litharge: the dross formed when lead is heated

Menez Mikêl: the Mont Saint-Michel of the hills of Arrée

quiver: a case for holding arrows

Quolibet: from the Latin *quod libet* – any question in philosophy or theology proposed as an exercise in argument or disputation.

Yeûn Elez: Breton for 'the marsh of the reeds'

Youdik: Breton for a soft mush or gruel; a hole leading to Hell

Historical Figures of the Twelfth Century

Abélard: Pierre Abélard (1079–1142). Scholastic philosopher and theologian; also known for his poetry and his celebrated love affair with Héloïse.

Aliénor (Eleanor) of Aquitaine (1122–1204): perhaps the most powerful woman in twelfth-century Europe. Queen of France (1137–52) by her marriage to Louis VII and Queen of England (1154–89) by her marriage to Henry II. Mother of the English Kings Richard I and John.

Bernard de Clairvaux (1091–1153): Cistercian monk and mystic, the founder and Abbot of the abbey of Clairvaux and one of the most influential churchmen of his time.

Conan III, Duke of Cornwall (1118–48): son of Duchess Ermengarde (see below). Married Mathilde, who bore him a daughter by the name of Berthe. Just before he died he declared his son Hoël illegitimate.

Conrad III: Germanic emperor (1138–52). In 1147 he took part in the Second Crusade with Louis VII.

Ermengarde, Duchess of Cornwall: Daughter of Foulques le Réchin. A cultivated and pious woman, she had great influence over her son Conan III. She helped the Cistercians establish themselves in Brittany. On the death of her son she went to join her brother in the Holy Land and ended her days in Jerusalem.

Geoffroy de Lèves: Bishop of Chartres at the time when this novel is set, and a friend of Abbé Suger (see below).

Guiomarch III: Vicomte of Léon in 1144.

Louis VII (1120–80): Capetian king of France who pursued a long rivalry, marked by recurrent warfare and continuous intrigue, with Henry II of England. Also called Louis Le Jeune.

Robert de Vitré: A friend of Conan III in his youth, Robert displeased him by his unjust attitude to his vassals. Conan seized Vitré, which Robert won back in 1144, after ten years of war.

Suger (1081–1151): Abbot and adviser to Louis VI and VII whose supervision of the rebuilding of the abbey church of Saint-Denis was instrumental in the development of the Gothic style of architecture. Acted as regent in 1147–9 while Louis VII was away on the Second Crusade.

Tanguy, Vicomte de Poher: Controlling the seigneury of Carhaix, Landélan, Châteauneuf-du-Faou and Huelgoat, making fifty-six parishes in all.

Thibaud (Theobald) IV (1093–1152): Count of Blois and of Chartres.